Two Girls, Two Dogs and a Campervan

a tale inspired by a true story

by Bea Sharif

First paperback edition April 2019

Edited by Lisa Howard
Cover design by Miladinka Milic
Book interior design by Tobi Carter

ISBN 978-0-578-49209-4 (paperback)
ISBN 978-0-578-49598-9 (hardback)
ISBN 978-0-578-49208-7 (ebook)

www.beasharif.com

Contents

Preface

I had never thought about writing a book until late last year.

Although we all believe we have a book in us, it never dawned on me to plunk myself down and write mine. But because traveling and experiencing nature are some of the most joyous experiences I've had, I realized I wanted to put pen to paper and share my tales of travel, placing them within the context of a fictional series that chronicles my most memorable journeys. This, the story of a California road trip I took in 2018 with my business partner/friend and her two adorable dogs, is the first of a six-part series.

I hope you'll travel along with me on my adventures as I share travel stories I've gathered throughout the decades, starting with my most recent California trip and ending with tales from my teens. Future books will chronicle my travels throughout South America, Africa, Asia, Europe and the US. Each book will jump back a decade, intertwining my travel adventures with relationships I've built with myself and others along the way.

Acknowledgments

With particular thanks to Bonita Inza and her two beautiful dogs—what a great time!

Thanks, too, to my entire family, especially my wonderful sister, Susie Saran, whose generosity and love for her pets knows no bounds.

Finally, a special mention to all the start-up founders who've yet to achieve your dreams of success—all of you who try, inspire me everyday.

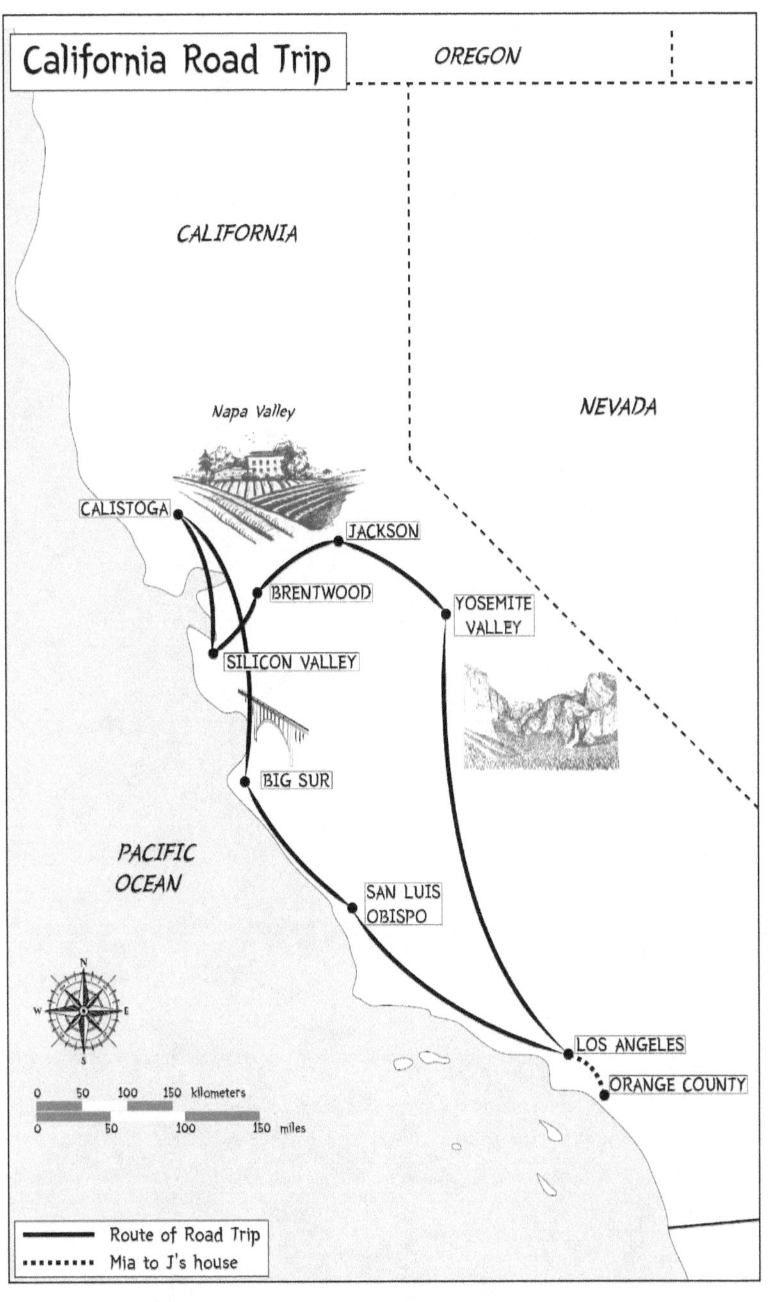

California Road Trip
OREGON
CALIFORNIA
NEVADA
Napa Valley
CALISTOGA
JACKSON
BRENTWOOD
YOSEMITE VALLEY
SILICON VALLEY
BIG SUR
PACIFIC OCEAN
SAN LUIS OBISPO
LOS ANGELES
ORANGE COUNTY
N
W
E
S
0   50   100   150   kilometers
0   50   100   150   miles
Route of Road Trip
Mia to J's house

Chapter 1

Co-Founders

'M A CO-FOUNDER of a tech start-up. Doesn't that sound great? But what does it mean, really? Many people think a co-founder is going to get rich soon. The common perception is co-founders are dreamers who work hard, are in their 20s and live in their parents' basement as they're scrambling to pitch their "great" idea or product to anybody who will listen. Eventually, they obtain funding from a Silicon Valley investor, and then after a few years of market penetration that scales up (i.e., consumers are buying into the idea or product and many more will in the future), co-founders sell their business or merge with a bigger fish. They've made it! These dreamers are now rich heroes of the venture capital and private equity world. (Venture capitalists are the "money people" who take big chances and believe in other people's ideas.) The co-founders are now living the dream—they've got their handsome million-dollar house, new Tesla(s) in the garage, a wine cellar with lots of expensive wines, a sailboat or yacht and lots of cool material things that for some mask a hidden sadness.

That scenario is what lots of people assume when they hear the word "co-founder." Those who've tried to be co-founders themselves and failed, however, know the reality of the situation: it starts with the dream and then involves having many coffees with people who have lots of money and consequently hearing rejections that are cordial but constant. If you are one of the lucky ones who gets an initial ("seed") round of funding, there's a daily excruciating grind of work to induce consumers to buy the product or idea ("market adoption"). If consumers adopt your product, great! But when those consumers *aren't* buying, you first ask yourself, "What's wrong?"

One side of your brain tells you that all you need to do is tweak or reconfigure something to get people to spend their money and then everything will be fine, and the other side of your brain says, "Oh, God, is this not going to work at all!" Then, after you've spent months of not wanting to give in to the fear that you're in the midst of a disaster, the day finally comes when you tell yourself and then your business partner(s) what everyone dreads hearing most: "It's not happening."

My business partner and co-founder J and I are in the middle of these two scenarios—we haven't "made it," and we haven't "failed." Yet. And we are not 20-somethings, we are 50-somethings. That's right: FIFTY-somethings. Neither of us live with our parents, and we both come out of the corporate world. We're successful—we've made money and saved money—and we've both vowed to never go back to corporate America.

Two years ago, we had an idea, received funding, built a technology product and launched it into the market. Very few people bought it, and now we're "stuck" because we don't agree with Alex, our financial co-founder (aka "the money guy"), on how to adjust our marketing plans. This is a big deal. So, we're not spending any money *and* we're not acquiring enough consumers…It's the classic chicken-or-the-egg scenario of which came first. I say, spend nothing, get nothing!

Don't get me wrong—Alex is a nice guy. In no way is he like some venture capital guys who yell or tell you what to do in a condescending manner. Although he does call us "the girls" sometimes, I'm sure he doesn't mean to imply that we don't know what we're doing. Still, J and I do get a laugh when we hear him refer to us as "the girls." Don't let anyone tell you there isn't gender bias in the venture capital industry, because there is and it's everywhere. But we're not complaining—we came from the corporate world, and it's pervasive there, too. We've dealt with gender bias throughout our careers and will never use it as an excuse.

Alex is a success story. As a young kid, he founded his own tech company without any outside investors, worked hard and made it big. Now in his 40s, he continues to work and invest in people and companies he takes an interest in. He has accrued everything that comes with success: the cars, the gorgeous house in Silicon Valley, the boat, the private plane…he's earned it all. We were lucky to have him at the start. But as with most start-ups, when things don't go according to plan, partners disagree on what to do next, and because Alex controls the purse strings, he's calling the shots.

At this point, most partners would have had "the talk" and would have said something along the lines of, "Well, we tried, and it didn't work. Time to shut it all down." Others might have said, "Stay the course! It's just a bump in the road." You can find thousands of books, articles, podcasts, etc. by founders and corporate executives describing how tough it is to get a business going and that if you need to "pivot" (this is a fancy word for "change course because the original idea isn't working"), just pivot. Yes, it's hard to pivot, but "Just do it!" is the advice you hear. This is easily said if you've ultimately overcome obstacles and become successful in the past. It's even more easily said if you've got money to reinvest in a new plan.

Knowing that Alex wants to move on, J and I are starting to work with other investors. This means lots more coffees, meetings and revising our pitch deck (that's our "asking for money" document). In the process, we're finding some potential financial co-founders who believe in what we're doing and who want to assume Alex's role, which is to say buy him out and invest in our revised plan. Exciting, yes? Well, not quite yet…

… Because timing is everything in business and in life, and the potential investors are not quite ready. Why? They're involved in another venture deal. In this environment, there are *always* deals upon deals. This deal in particular needs to be negotiated for an IPO ("Initial Public Offering"), and let's just say it's slow going. It may not even happen. An IPO is a super huge event for *any* company—it means that you've really made it and that the initial investors will net lots of money.

If they are able to secure their IPO, that would be an extraordinary second chance for us. *If* it happens. J and I really like these guys—they have experience, they like our product and our new business plan, and they're strategic, meaning they're uniquely a good fit for our tech product. And the bottom line is we keep our baby alive.

As co-founders of a tech start-up, when you develop an idea and the initial plan doesn't work, you are typically afforded one shot only. Here, with our interested investors, we potentially have a lifeline to change up the marketing plan and try again. It's rare to earn that second chance. If J and I honestly felt like we'd put forth a good effort but with a bad product, we'd let our baby go, releasing it into the pile of start-up failures. We would not be alone in doing so. But we still believe in our idea, we're still willing to "live and breathe the company," meaning do nothing else, and we have others on our radar who also see the interesting prospects our tech product offers and who are willing to back up our idea with money. Now we just have to be patient.

When we ask the investors how long it will take for them to complete their other deal, they say, "Six months." Six months?! What will we do for *six months*? It'd be one thing if the venture was a sure thing, but it's not—it's a maybe. And we know that as is the case with all good intentions, a "Maybe" usually becomes "Sorry it didn't work out."

What will J and I do? We're stuck in what I think of as "start-up quicksand." It's a frustrating place to be, because there's a lot of uncertainty. Do we have faith and wait for these guys to get their other deal done? Or do we fold our business today and move on and start considering—I don't want to even *think* about the next words—getting regular jobs? Oh, please, no. No…

We schedule a board meeting via a conference call to vote on whether to keep the company alive (albeit in a dormant stage) for the next six months while we wait to see if the interested investors will be able to fund their investment in our company. This would mean six more months of J and I pulling money from our respective savings accounts, something that would definitely add stress to our lives. We both want to start earning income again, and soon.

Did I fail to mention earlier that co-founders at this level rarely get paid a salary? That lack of salary means that we are draining our retirement funds each and every month and have been for the past two years. I mean, how much do we really believe in this idea? Enough to continue to risk our retirement? These are the kinds of questions that we frequently ask each other. It's not easy to bet on yourself. But when you believe, you take risks. This is the price we pay to dream. Call us crazy (some already do), but we don't think we're crazy—we've been afforded the opportunity to bet on ourselves, and we're going for it. I guess that's why J and I get along so well as friends and also business partners.

Alex is willing to wait for six months—after all, he's not worried about living without a salary seeing as he's running another company. (Remember what I said about venture deals on top of venture deals?) He votes yes to continue keeping our business alive for another six months, although in the meantime, we can only spend what's necessary on the business.

I've worked in and out of the corporate world for the past thirty years. (Sometimes I've been in the office; sometimes I've been out of it traveling the world.) Although I was successful in the corporate environment, I was only successful when I dedicated an unrelenting amount of time to my job. I was a workaholic while employed, zeroing in solely on the work at hand. Eventually, that became an unsustainable situation for me, so I would quit my job and sought out adventures, traveling to other countries for months on end. This is how I was able to reinvigorate myself in mind, body and spirit.

I've never been drawn to titles or money—instead, I've always wanted to explore and have adventures and create memorable traveling experiences. I couldn't care less about what kind of car I drive or how big my house is or overly luxurious things like that. I recognized the pitfalls of striving to own material things long ago and I decided that I wasn't going to spend my life focusing on having those trinkets. Travel has offered me a lifetime of experiences that I could never have attained if I had spent years working sixty- to eighty-hour weeks without any substantial breaks of weeks or months.

I also have a close-knit circle of family and friends who love me, cheer for me and support me in many ways, and when you have that, life presents you with a sense of security and a safety net—you know that everything will somehow be okay. So I, too, vote yes to wait for six months in the hopes that the investors come through for us. In the end, it isn't a hard decision for me.

J also votes yes, making it unanimous. On this matter, at least, the three of us are all aligned.

I've known J (short for Jennifer) for ten years, and I know there's no way she would turn her back on this possibility, either. She's worked her entire life in the corporate world and has dealt with all of the political gamesmanship that comes with executive-level positions. She definitely is averse to going back to that lifestyle. She's a powerhouse with strong opinions and limitless resilience. Some coworkers have considered her to be difficult, but that's not what she is, not really—she just won't mindlessly follow like an obedient sheep. Some would call her an alpha female, strong and fearless, but those are just labels. She has more depth than that, a depth that also showcases vulnerability.

Like most business partners and co-founders, we're very different when it comes to our personalities, our interests and how we address issues. I make quick decisions. I have a B.S. detector with a mile's reach, and I will sometimes call people out on their B.S. I have very little patience for idiots, fools and superficiality. I can multitask with fierceness and balance ten to twenty things at once… though admittedly with my share of mistakes along the way. "Making mistakes is all part of the process," I say to myself. I don't mind stumbling as I go. As long as I keep moving forward (whether figuratively or literally), that's the key. Overthinking any issue just slows me down. For me, it's more important to keep moving than to stop, deliberate and address every item to make sure it's perfect.

J, on the other hand, will go very deep when she finds a subject that interests her, and she's tenacious in her efforts to educate herself thoroughly. Given enough time (and if she had an inkling of an interest in doing so), I believe she could crack nuclear codes. The flip side is that she can overthink a problem, overanalyze inconsequential matters and create more complexities than necessary. This is why we're compatible as business partners and make each other laugh as friends.

So now it's official: our company is in a holding pattern for six months. What do we do now? J and I need a brainstorming session. Neither of us are one to sit around—whatever we do, we'll be proactive. Maybe we'll conduct more research or talk to more potential investors (even though that idea makes me sick to my stomach). We'll do *something*, because you never know when or where the next opportunity may arise or who may know someone who knows someone who can help. These are the things you say to yourself so that you don't feel lazy or unproductive.

Chapter 2

SoCal

J **AND I LIVE** in southern California, in two counties adjacent to each other on the west coast: Los Angeles (LA) and Orange County. In general, both are well-known for their sunny and mild, temperate climate, diverse geography, sandy coastal beaches, nearby desert landscapes/national parks such as Joshua Tree and Death Valley, and mountain ranges that allow for hiking, skiing and snowboarding in the winter. The two counties are only fifty miles apart. Still, they're very different.

Given their close proximity, you might ask, how can they be so different? Some of the differences are subtle; some are striking. The differences lie in how the two counties are laid out and in the make-up of their respective cultures, energy and overall vibe of the small cities within the counties. As a Midwesterner, I initially hated LA, but over the course of a year, I began to get it. I've lived in both LA and Orange County for extended periods of time and love them both, but as I've grown older, I find that Orange County fits my personality today.

LA is a poster board for the entertainment community. It prides itself on being bigger than life and showcases huge billboards all over the city, from alongside the freeways to atop major boulevards such as Wilshire and Sunset. LA evokes an immersive sense of magic. "If you dream big enough and are willing to work hard enough," LA seems to be saying, "then really huge things can happen for you." The city fuels a great sense of opportunity and the possibility that you can make monumental achievements across a variety of industries, but especially in the entertainment world. That world in particular ignites creativity, hope and the feeling that you can succeed in unprecedented ways.

You can feel and hear the essence of this wondrous environment everywhere you go. I remember the first time I drove on the 405. I exited onto Wilshire Boulevard and was immediately faced with a very large billboard right in front of me. As I was driving, I kept looking up—I couldn't take my eyes off of it, not until I had passed it by. The billboard was advertising a summer movie about to hit theaters. The size of it was imposing; I felt like I was in another world. Driving along Sunset Boulevard, you encounter the same feeling again and again as you see billboards of A-list movie and TV stars who've made it big. Seeing those tangible, imposing symbols every day infused a feeling of "keep working, keep reaching," not for the money or fame, but for a personal sense of achievement, sort of competing with myself to do more.

The culture is held together by and centered on the gorgeous sunny days. At times, it feels like you're in a themed playground, a place where limitless possibilities are there for you if your imagination can match the opportunity. The immersive energy of LA promotes a sense of knowing no boundaries… it's an organic experience you can feel everywhere. The sensations are in coffee shops, restaurants, car washes, sporting events, hiking trails—yes, even as you're hiking in Runyon Canyon. It's in the air, it's in the water… at times, there's an indescribable exuberance that leads to excitement. I've not encountered another city with this essence.

Set amongst all of this grand energy are the coastal cities of Santa Monica and Venice with their iconic beach counter-culture history. They have an underlying vitality strongly focused on wellness, offering a large yogic, meditational, nutritional and spiritual community that is at the epicenter of some innovative and interesting new companies, studios and traditional and non-traditional wellness centers. This is what really excites J.

But despite its illustrious image, there's a *lot* wrong with LA. Where to begin? With the high taxes and cost of living? Or what about the homelessness, extreme traffic and scooters that litter entire neighborhoods? (I won't say too many bad things about the scooters, though—the people who founded the scooter companies figured out how to address a major transportation issue, and I give them lots of credit for doing so. Someday, I do hope someone creates an esthetically pleasing rack to store all of those aluminum-powered street vehicles that are currently scattered around like loose change—there's another idea for the future.)

The single biggest negative about LA—and it's one that no one talks about—is that it's hard to make new friends outside of your own network. A lot of that certainly has to do with the fact that we all are in our cars most of the time, but it's also true that most Angelenos make little effort to widen their social circles—after a certain amount of time, we fall into a there's-no-sense-in-trying mindset. I'm certainly guilty of this as well. It's simply hard to reach out when most of your time is spent in your car, at work or with your existing friends. There are exceptions to this, of course, but speaking for myself, my friends are the friends I had prior to arriving in southern California.

While LA is a beacon of aspirational grandeur sprawling across a landscape of immense and diverse possibilities, Orange County quietly lies to the south, content to allow its northern neighbor to accept all of the attention and publicity it so craves. To describe Orange County versus LA in just a few words, it might be fair to say that it's a suburban versus urban mentality. (I use the term "urban" very loosely when it comes to describing LA, because it's a relative scale. Honestly, there's nothing much urban about it if you need to drive everywhere.) In many ways, Orange County is the opposite of LA County: it's less diverse (although that's changing as more Asian and Hispanic populations move in), its pace is slower, it's quieter and it's cleaner.

Going south along the coastline, you have Huntington Beach, home to Surf City and The Beach Boys, where world-class surfers from around the world come to catch the waves. Farther south is Newport Beach, the nouveau community with many yacht and sailboat harbors. Even farther south lies Laguna Beach, a little gem of a town. It's an upscale artist community that's trying to maintain its sweet coastal charm. As you enter Laguna Beach from the north, you're immediately struck by all of the bougainvillea along Pacific Coast Highway (PCH)—the roadside is a coral-pink haven of enchantment, with flowers and blooming plants everywhere.

As it commonly occurs in most of southern California along the coast, tourists rush these hotspots during the spring and summer months, but during fall and winter, it's heavenly. Laguna Beach is small enough that you can actually walk around town. Depending on the time of year, the air will be filled with scents of jasmine and hibiscus in the spring; wisteria, gardenias, lilacs and lavender in the summer; and plumeria in the fall. If you're in the higher elevations, you also have one of the most stunning views of the Pacific Ocean anywhere in California.

But just as it is in LA, I find it's hard to make real friends in Orange County, too, because the same mentality applies here: few people really try. And the same drawbacks that exist in LA are experienced in Orange County: traffic issues, a super-high cost of living, an ever-increasing homeless population, etc. Along the coast, the biggest negatives are a lack of diversity and—for me, at least—not enough interesting restaurants. Though I must say, the food trucks in Costa Mesa and Santa Ana are killer!

At times, I really miss LA… but you can't have it all, and the peacefulness I experience farther south outweighs the negatives. Besides, with LA just fifty miles away, when the mood strikes me and I want to eat at a great restaurant or visit friends, it's an acceptable drive if I plan to go around non-peak traffic times. (During peak times, forget it!)

While J feels at home along LA's coastal scene, I've discovered that the relative calm and quiet nature of Laguna Beach suits me much more. I like sleeping in my little bungalow and *not* worrying about the sounds of police helicopters hovering over my neighborhood, wondering what's going on and checking my Twitter feed to see what criminal activity is happening nearby. I like *not* having to agonize about parking my car on the street and worrying if it'll be broken into or keyed overnight. I like *not* having to check signs to see if my side of the street is being cleaned tomorrow and I need to move my car at 7 a.m. I like *not* having a thirty-minute drive just to go five miles. Those are the kinds of annoyances I remember putting up with when I was living in LA, and I'm happy to be rid of them.

These days, if anything about Orange County annoys me, it's that I may be bored.

Chapter 3

Nature

I LOVE DOGS AND have been thinking about getting one for years. Over and over, I keep telling myself it's now time to make that commitment. I even have a breed and a sweet name picked out. But a heavy workload, constant travel and long periods spent away from home have kept preventing me from being a dog owner. I feel it wouldn't be fair to the dog, who would wind up being home alone and sad or in a doggie motel. So, I enjoy others' dogs, especially when I spend time at my sister's home or at J's.

J is a big dog lover and has two rescues. She's an awesome mommy! Sure, maybe she's a bit too hovering and protective at times, but hey, as a non-pet owner, who am I to judge? J's dogs are spoiled with the best organic dog food, vitamins and oils one can buy, and they're pampered with weekly spa days, doggie social groups and meetups. I would almost sign up to have their lives! Being around J and her dogs has given me a new appreciation of all the New Age activities and programs out there for pets. Living in California, J's in good company—the one thing that's universal across California is the love that dog owners have for their pets and how welcomed they are by commercial and hospitality establishments throughout the state.

Like many Californians, J has also been practicing yoga for decades. You just know certain women are yogis when you see them—they have those yoga bodies, the long, lean, healthy ones. J looks like that. A long-time vegetarian, she also has a keen interest in non-traditional forms of wellness and spirituality.

As a woman without kids who's recently become single, J is learning how to live a life of independence and solo discovery. She's become an avid consumer of wellness and spiritual books, blogs, podcasts and YouTube videos about self-help strategies, and she loves sharing them with me. I'll wake up to all sorts of text messages and emails with links to articles, videos, blogs, you name it. She'll ask me to please take a look at it and we can talk about it later. I think, *Yuck!*

After a few days, she'll kindly ask if I've taken a look. Most of the time, I've procrastinated in the hopes that she'll forget, but she doesn't forget. She never forgets. So, then I'll open a link, read an article or view a video. Usually the videos are made by someone who has a terribly high-pitched voice and who's really difficult to follow. Sometimes there are references to moons, saving yourself, following your dreams, feeling more confident, understanding your strengths and weaknesses, setting some goals and/or there's a purpose for you.

Sometimes there's a discernible message, but even then, it just takes too long for the person to get to the point. One day, I might need someone to explain my impatience with it all. Is there something wrong with me? Maybe, but then again, I feel I've got to go with what works for me, and pretty much none of those links J sends me resonate. But similar messages do influence so many others, and we all need to discover more about ourselves in our own way.

My way—I look to travel and specifically nature for solace and a divinity. I value the solemnness and joy that exploration, nature and outdoor activities provide, whether that's long road trips, hiking, backpacking, camping or snowboarding. All of those activities always lead me to a sense of balance, especially if I'm able to do them in gorgeous settings. That's what creates *my* center of gravity. I've summited Mount Kilimanjaro in Africa, hiked trails along Mont Blanc in

France, Aconcagua and Fitz Roy in Argentina, Patagonia in Chile, the Camino de Santiago trail in Spain, and the Ngorongoro Crater in Kenya and Tanzania, among many others. I've been truly humbled by these experiences in so many ways.

I've seen the depths of poverty, experienced the generosity, kindness and hospitality of hundreds and pushed myself to demanding physical and mental challenges. All the while, it's in these settings that I've been fortunate to meet complete strangers in foreign lands, experience our love of travel and nature, and thereafter maintain long-lasting friendships.

In my opinion, traveling unlocks the mind, heart and soul, allowing for self-exploration like no other alternative can. It and nature infuse me with the sense of wonderment, wellness and self-purpose. Nothing gives me more gratification or envelops me with more childlike joy than testing my will on a mountain or hiking a strenuous trail or riding along a road less traveled.

I have an independent lifestyle—no kids, no dogs and I'm single—so I can pick up and leave at any time. I cherish my independence and never take it for granted. The areas I have traveled through are some of the most precious corners of the world! They're windows into unimaginable beauty, and I have them forever stamped into my brain. When things aren't right on any given day, I can reach back to those memories and feelings to remind me that life is short and that I shouldn't sweat the small, petty nonsense. Nature is what I need for my self-nurturing: it's my life coach, it's my church, it's my *om*.

Chapter 4

The Dogs

AFTER THIS WEEK'S decision to suspend our company for six months, I arrive at J's house ready to start brainstorming on what we should focus on doing in the meantime. It was a great drive getting there on the 405 North, with little traffic at 10 a.m. My music playlist on the way included Foals, Arcade Fire, Milky Chance, Radiohead, Cage the Elephant—the kind of music that boosts me into a joyous place of "life is good." This is the one benefit of car solitude: you have plenty of time to listen to music and I love all types of music. I'm a morning person and have high energy levels in the early hours, so I'm feeling "ready to go."

I walk up to the front door of J's two-story Spanish Tudor house with a spring in my step. I ring the doorbell… and she opens the door in tears. I immediately think the worst: *Oh, no—her dog Stormy died!*

Doggie deaths are so sad. I've already experienced one with my sister earlier this month, and it's incredibly emotional.

I gently place my hands on her arms and ask, "What's wrong? What happened?" It's Striker, she tells me. Her 3-year-old Vizsla mutt has jumped off of her second-floor balcony and broken his front leg. I feel my mouth drop open for what feels like a full minute—I can't believe what I just heard, although given her tears, this is obviously real. There's already been quite a bit of drama related to that sweet dog. I thought that had all passed, but apparently, I was wrong. "Where is he?"

She sniffles. "At the vet hospital. He's just come out of surgery—his front right leg broke in half at the elbow. X-rays confirmed no other injuries, but still, it's a very severe break. He needs pins and he'll be in a cast for six weeks." She's sobbing so hard that her nose is bright red.

I feel like my jaw has now dropped to my knees as I keep trying to picture the dog flying over the balcony and landing in her yard. What was he thinking?? I don't want to ask too many questions because J is clearly traumatized, but this is bizarre.

Throughout the months she's had Striker, she has discovered that he's a very emotionally dependent dog. That's certainly not unusual for a Vizsla rescue, poor thing. He has deep attachment issues and does not leave J for a moment. She has likewise become intensely attached to him, especially bonding with him during the early weeks when she brought him home and he was getting used to his new environment. You could say that both have co-dependency issues.

She told me more about how it happened. Apparently, she was upstairs cleaning the second-floor patio balcony off of her master bedroom while Striker (as usual) was nearby. Suddenly and without any warning, Striker ran onto the patio, flew off of the patio furniture, sailed through the air like Super Dog and landed on her lawn. Thank goodness he landed in the grassy nook.

"Maybe he was scared of the vacuum cleaner," she manages to gasp out as she continues to weep. "I don't know..."

"Oh, my goodness, I'm so sorry," I say, still in shock. I follow her inside as she goes to put on her shoes and get her keys.

"Can you stay with Stormy while I go get Striker?" she asks.

"Of course I can!" I say. "He's already being released today, so that's a very good sign," I add, trying to offer some comfort.

"Yes, I hope so," she says softly, then pauses for a moment. Her eyes threaten to flood with tears again. She visibly gathers herself and gives me a grateful hug before stepping out the door.

I'm still thinking to myself, *Why, why, why did he decide to just jump off of a balcony? Was he scared? Was he playing and didn't realize what he had just done? Was he trying to get his mommy's attention?* Major head-scratcher.

J leaves, and I find myself dog-sitting Stormy, a 13-year-old Vizsla rescue mutt who's part Vizsla and part Labrador Retriever. He's an old soul of a dog with numerous growths and ailments, and he's completely deaf. He also has the sweetest hazel eyes imaginable, eyes surrounded by gray and chocolate-brown hair. I wonder what Stormy was doing when all hell broke loose? He doesn't appear to be too bothered by the recent chain of events. We head into the living room, where he plops himself down onto his doggie bed. Good boy, good boy. Gotta love a quiet, chill dog.

Later, I take Stormy out for his business. He's a bit slow on his feet, especially if he's going uphill or climbing stairs. Sometimes he literally just stops in the middle of the street or sidewalk and refuses to move any farther. He's like an old man saying, "I've done what I came to do! Now, just let me relax a bit before I move any more." Luckily, J has treats for these instances, and I always carry them with me if I'm assisting in dog-walking tasks. The routine goes like this: I place a treat in front of Stormy, and he begins to get up. Once he's up, the treat is provided, and he's moving again, albeit sluggishly. Once he starts to move, he's good all the way home.

There have been instances where we've forgotten the treats, and getting him back up is a long and arduous exercise of pretending we have food, pulling hard on the leash, trying to pick him up but being unable to do so, running in front of him to try to get him to move…Nothing works. You just have to wait. At times, it can be downright embarrassing if other dog owners walk by, leash in hand while Stormy stubbornly takes a lay right in the middle of the street or sidewalk. Who's leading who? The answer to that is pretty obvious: he's calling the shots, and when he's ready, he'll move and we'll get to move, too. He'll look at us with his beautiful hazel eyes when that time comes and give us the signal that yes, we can all move again. For us to pretend that we can move him before he's ready is futile. All of this means that a normal twenty-minute dog walk takes nearly double that with Stormy, it's just slow. Dogs are amazing, especially as they get older. They're pretty much the one in control.

While I wait for J to return with Striker, I'm preparing a list of items we need to think about as our company is in its state of suspended animation, so to speak. How do we manage this period? What other investors could we speak to? What more could we do to market our product without spending anything? What more should we research? Is there something we haven't done? Should we do some street-level marketing, should we do some online surveys…We want to keep exploring any and all avenues.

A couple of hours later

The door opens, and here comes Striker and J. His right front leg from his paw up to his body is covered with bandages, he's barely hopping along on his three good legs, and his eyes are bloodshot and dazed. He was obviously given drugs for his surgery. J also has bloodshot eyes from crying and the shock of seeing her dog go flying over the balcony for no apparent reason. She's also clearly weary from lack of sleep.

"How's he doing?" I ask with great sympathy.

She cradles him a little closer. "The doctors think he'll be okay, although the leg will need time to heal. Hopefully he'll be able to fully use it again—I have to monitor his progress."

I nod and follow her as she takes him upstairs, puts him in her bed and throws a blanket over him. When I tell her I'll spend the night, she's thankful. I go into her kitchen to see what's in the fridge, see that it's empty and call for take-out. An order of veggie pasta and a salad is ordered into Postmates and delightedly a quick delivery of our food is at the door. We eat, share a bottle of wine and engage in whispering conversation on her bed with Striker lying quietly near us. J just stares at him while continuing to rub his forehead. His eyes are closed, he's whimpering and I'm sure appreciating his mommy's loving touch.

Nearby, Stormy is completely unfazed, curled up in his daybed in the corner. It's an early night, it's been a long day. I head over to the guest room and Stormy gets up and follows behind. I guess he's sleeping near me tonight.

The following morning, Striker looks somewhat better—he's hopping on his three legs and dragging the bandaged leg along, injured but seemingly instilled with a sense of resiliency. It's quite amazing, really. He intently watches J as he's lying on his daybed downstairs, following her every move with his eyes. Stormy remains in his own world. I'm not sure what he's thinking, but he obviously is showing no sympathy for Striker. Interesting dynamics there.

Whatever work I wanted to accomplish here clearly isn't going to happen, but that's okay—at this point, Striker needs J's undivided attention and TLC. Before I head back home, J and I decide to take both dogs out for their morning walks. I've got Stormy, she's got Striker. As I step out the door, I look back and up to the bedroom balcony. Boy, that was a big fall; I can't believe it was only two days ago as I marvel at Striker, who's hopping down the road on his three good legs. Pretty crazy!

I look at Stormy who's by my side, also looking up at the balcony as well. I wonder what he knows. I wonder what he's thinking. Doggie Mystery!

Chapter 5

Rejuvenate

One month later

JAND THE DOGS are coming to visit, and I'm looking forward to seeing Striker's progress. It's their first trip outside of Los Angeles since Striker's Super Dog accident.

I live in a single-story, two-bedroom, wood-framed beach cottage with no stairs. A lack of stairs will make it easier for both dogs these days! Like most cottages in the area, mine was built in the 1940s and has an old artistic charm that's unique to this area. Laguna Beach takes great pride in making sure that building developers adhere to strict codes that keep the town's historic charm intact. The best part about my property, however, is the garden: it's a small back patio lined by a red-tipped shrub called photinia for privacy, and it's filled with lilacs, poppies, birds of paradise, jasmine, roses and a fountain that provides gentle sounds of cascading water. Only a block from the beach, it's a perfectly tranquil setting.

There's a knock at the door, and I hear J happily shout, "We're here!!" I see them all through my living room window as I rush to open the door. There he is! Striker is now wearing a big plastic white cone over his head and bouncing around on three legs as he drags along his bandaged fourth.

"Oh!" I gasp happily as I reach down and embrace him. I give him a big hug and kiss. He looks back at me with his rather pitiful "I'm sick" eyes, but according to J, he's been healing well.

She's taken great care of him, spending countless hours researching the best nutrition, medicines and non-traditional ointments to assist with his recovery. All of his care—and the cost of it—has taken its toll on her. His surgery was damn expensive! She's shelled out thousands of dollars for the hospital, veterinarian, medicines, organic food, CBD oils, vitamins and organic honey. I know those costs are even tougher given our current no-salary situation, and I can't help but think in the back of my mind, *This may be why I don't have any dogs at the moment...*

Then there's Stormy, who pushes by all of us as we're gathered at the door and starts going in and out of each room in the house. J tells me that Stormy has not provided much sympathy while Striker has been going through his recovery stage—he just does his own thing and tries to remind J that he needs attention, too. I love Stormy, so I run after him and into the kitchen, where I bend down and stare into his aging eyes and give him his own big hug and kiss.

J looks tired—she hasn't been sleeping well. She's clearly internalizing guilt. I tell her, "Shit happens! It was an accident. We'll never really understand why Striker jumped, but he's in a great home and he's got a mommy who will go above and beyond for his well-being and care." *Way* above and *way* beyond.

Because of the hour-and-a-half drive it took for J to get to my place, a dog walk is in order, so we head to the beach. Unlike many SoCal beaches, the little cove near my house allows dogs after 6 p.m. If they're in the mood to play, Striker and Stormy will be able to roll around in the sand and water. What dog doesn't love that? It will be interesting to see how Striker will respond to the beach given his bad leg. As usual, J has Striker and I've got Stormy. J hands me a couple of poop bags.

As we walk, we talk and share some of our current concerns. My biggest one is feeling blah and unproductive; her biggest one is wanting to make sure that Striker recovers as fully as possible.

For the past few weeks, J and I have filled our days with trying to find more opportunities, creating a list of additional potential investors should the ones we're waiting on fall through, and meeting with some in person over coffees. It feels like a lot of busy work, but then again, it all may pay off—you can never predict how things might turn out. Being part of a start-up requires throwing a lot of balls into the air and keeping abreast of competitors and the marketplace. The process is a slog; discipline is absolutely required. Some days are definitely harder than others.

I tell her I've been thinking of going for a short weekend hiking trip nearby. I've been researching the national parks within a day's drive that I haven't yet visited and found a few candidates, including Joshua Tree (two hours away), Death Valley (another short drive) or even Monument Valley in southern Utah (not nearly as close). The last one would require more time, true, but it's very high on my list of parks to visit. My key considerations are that I want to hike, I want to be able to camp so that I can hear the sounds of nature as I sleep, and I want a road trip. I need to rejuvenate myself, to take those slow upward steps and experience a renewed sense of enlightenment. I know that this is how I will mentally recover and get back to the core of me.

"But you know where I *really* want to go?" I ask her rhetorically. "It finally hit me last night." I pause to smile as J waits expectantly. "Yosemite! That's where I'm going!"

I've never been to Yosemite, and climbing Half Dome at 8,800 feet is on my bucket list. I continue to have the bug to summit iconic peaks, and Yosemite would be perfect. Of all of my travels, climbing Kilimanjaro may have been the best trip ever. Seeing Africa and its wildlife, backpacking for five days… everyone who's done it will tell you it alters your thinking for the rest of your life. My appreciation for nature was elevated by that trip and everything it taught me. If you can tackle all of the obstacles related to that climb, you can address and break down any future fears by using what Kilimanjaro taught you: take things a step at a time, never look back or down, and know that you have a support system of colleagues and friends (who, in the case of Kilimanjaro, are the porters, who are perhaps the most important companions of all). It's a beautiful metaphor for life.

For this trip, I tell her, I am planning on going solo or maybe finding a hiking club to go with so that I can meet new people. Either way, I just need to get out of town. I'm in need of some mental downtime, with no fuss and no stress, just a few days of hiking and camping.

J tells me she's been thinking of taking a spa weekend and asks if I want to go along. "Nope," I say quickly. I'm not interested in sitting in a luxurious resort wearing a robe and being pampered. I mean, if I'd been on a five- or six-day backpacking trip and I was filthy and in need of a good massage or facial, the spa idea would be great. But for it to be the highlight of my weekend? No, that idea doesn't excite me. I'd rather take a hot bath on my own. She's disappointed, but there's no way.

She also tells me she's been invited to a high-school reunion party in northern California (NoCal), which is where she was born and raised. She asks me to come with her, but I *really* don't want to attend someone else's reunion. I don't even go to mine! That's another "Nope." Her ideas are falling very flat very quickly. I'm one to quickly say no rather than string someone along. It's okay—she knows me well and is accustomed to my prompt and definite responses.

We get to the beach cove. Striker stays near J. No running, bouncing or hopping—he just stares up at J and looks over at Stormy. He sees other dogs, too, but he doesn't want to partake in any doggie playing or friendly sniffing. It's clear that given his current condition, he's not emotionally ready for company.

Stormy's not enjoying the beach much, either. What a shame! He takes a couple of steps and then plops himself down on the sand. No walking around or running about in the water. Bummer. I look over at J and shrug. "They're not in the mood." She nods in agreement, looking as disappointed as I feel. We head back to the house.

At the house, we continue our conversation over glasses of wine. After a few rounds, J says she wants to go hiking, too, and *with* the dogs. Now, I've known J for ten years, and I have never heard her talk about hiking, camping, the outdoors, nature or anything of the like. She takes five-star vacations, stays at luxury hotels, travels on first-class flights and dines at top-notch restaurants. Even *considering* doing anything outdoors that doesn't involve swanky lodgings is a huge stretch for her. I'm looking at her like she's lost her mind.

Don't get me wrong—I love J. She's an awesome friend. But... her dogs, too? On a hiking trip? With her currently three-and-a-half legged dog and her poor aging dog with plenty of ailments of his own? And she's not much of a hiker herself. She's a walker, yes; a hiker, no. I try to visualize how this would work. I just can't see her and the dogs in a tent. To put it plainly, some trips aren't for everybody. This would be one of those trips.

But somehow—and I'm not sure how we got there except for the fact that after a bottle of wine things always tend to get more flexible—we agree to merge our two trips and combine hiking and camping in Yosemite with a spa day and her reunion party. We get out our laptops and start pounding out an itinerary with the following parameters: 1) the dogs are coming, 2) we'll be gone for ten to twelve days, 3) it's a road trip, 4) I'm happy to drive given I have a Jeep Wrangler and 5) J will attend the reunion party.

She throws out some retreat/resort ideas: how about San Diego or Palm Springs? Neither strikes me as appealing, which is fine since neither is on the way to Yosemite or northern California. I reiterate that we are headed north. "Oh, right," she mutters. At that point, the wine is really kicking in, and we decide to put our planning on hold. We agree that I'll handle the first half of the trip, the part that will see us going to Yosemite (including finding a camping site and getting any necessary permits), and she'll coordinate the second half of the trip.

Right now, I look over at the dogs. They've foregone their doggie beds and instead have each found their own comfy spots on separate couches. Sand they tracked in from the beach is everywhere. *Great,* I can't help but think.

The sound of J laughing draws my eyes back to her. "They're so cute!" she says with a giggle. "Auntie Mia, this will be so much fun!" Of course, that's coming from a dog owner to a non-dog owner. Do *I* really want a doggie road trip?

Chapter 6

Planning

OUR TRIP IS just four weeks away, and I'm getting really excited about Yosemite. My travel juices are flowing as I'm reading up on the hiking trails, especially Half Dome. It's on many "greatest hikes and climbs in the world" lists. Every hiker likes to challenge their own abilities at times, whether the challenge comes in the form of elevation, length or type of terrain. Summiting Half Dome would be very meaningful. It's a non-technical hike of approximately seventeen miles and takes between ten to twelve hours to complete. It's very popular, too, so popular that a few years ago, the national park started implementing a lottery permit process. Because I've already missed the pre-season lottery dates, my only shot now at Half Dome will be snagging one of the fifty daily permits issued forty-eight hours prior to the hike. It's a long shot for sure.

In addition to Half Dome, I'm also reading up on the best campgrounds, their pluses and minuses, the overall history of the park, etc. I've scoured a number of Yosemite-specific sites as well as the Yosemite National Park website, watched YouTube videos about the trails and have been following some Instagram travel influencers who've posted about Yosemite. I'm trying to research and capture as much information as possible. Normally, I don't plan too much in advance because the idea of discovery and exploration is much more appealing when it's organic, but since Yosemite is a hugely popular destination and we're taking dogs—and trying to pull things together at the last minute—my usual habits won't work. A lot of forethought and planning is definitely required for this particular trip! Just showing up or winging it at Yosemite won't work. It would, in fact, be a disaster.

In the wake of our initial thoughts about our joint trip, J has added wine tasting in Napa Valley (which a friend will help coordinate) and going to Big Sur (which is another superb hiking location). Our road trip is really starting to take shape! We'll have lots of variety and enough of what we each like to do. We're also going to meet up with our co-founder Alex while in the San Francisco area—it'll be a nice chance to have coffee and catch up in person.

The current itinerary is:

- Hiking: Three days, four nights in Yosemite
- J's reunion: One day, one night in NoCal
- Silicon Valley – lunch with Alex: Afternoon
- Calistoga – spa and wine tasting: Two days, two nights
- Big Sur hiking: Two days, two nights
- Driving days: Two days (there and back)

After reading up on numerous camping options, I've narrowed our preferred campgrounds to being in one of the Upper, Lower or North Pines areas in Yosemite Valley. Those campgrounds are near Half Dome Village and are a central location, plus their proximity to some great hiking trails (including the few that allow dogs) makes them perfect.

When I go on Yosemite's website to research and reserve a campsite, everything is booked. Not *one* site is available—reservations must be made far, far in advance. More time spent reading and going onto chatrooms tells me that I need to visit the website every day and look for cancellations as they are posted in real time. This will be my main focus for the next few weeks, because I've *got* to get us into one of these campgrounds. Clearly, we are a little behind given our dates, but we'll do the best we can. I want to be in the valley! Plan B is…is… Well, I'm not going to worry about that right now. We're visiting during the spring, so I'm thinking alternative sites should be available if needed. Fingers crossed.

I'm working on our meals, too, seeing as J's not much of a cook. Both of our diets have restrictions: I'm gluten-free with some dairy issues, and she's a vegetarian. Typically, I just eat once a day and have some very light snacks, if any. Breakfast is not my thing—my body generally doesn't like food in the morning. On this trip, though, I will be hiking, so I'm going to adjust my meals accordingly and add oatmeal and eggs to the menu. I've decided I'll go vegetarian as well just to make grocery shopping easier. It's only a few days…no big deal.

The one thing that *is* a big deal for me is my one morning cup of coffee—it's what gets my day going. Specifically, my mornings start with an almond milk latte, and it has to be a good one. I need it! Otherwise, things that would not normally annoy me *will* begin to irk me. I just read up on a coffee shop in Half Dome Village, so if we're lucky enough to snag one of our preferred campsites, the coffee shop would be within walking distance. That's an added luxury I'd take. Not exactly "roughing it" this time!

Lots of planning is under way: prepping the menu, searching for recipes, checking Instagram postings for ideas, thinking about what needs to be bought (and where and when), pulling out all of my hiking gear and camping equipment, setting up my tent (i.e., confirming I have all the pieces) and airing out my sleeping bag. I need to check with J about her tent, too. If she doesn't already have what she needs (and I'm guessing she doesn't), she needs to start buying some of her equipment.

It's a Friday afternoon three weeks before our trip when J calls. "I've been doing some research and thinking," she begins. "What do you think about renting a campervan?"

I have never, ever thought about a campervan, actually; I don't know anything about them. "Why?" I ask.

She says that she wants to rent a campervan for the entire road trip, a suggestion that's met with silence on my part. "Hello...?" she prompts me after more seconds pass by.

"I'm thinking..." I say. I know my expression is a befuddled one. *She doesn't want to camp outdoors*, I think. *It's just too much for her to go from five-star traveling girl to camping-out cave girl.*

"Just take a look at this," she says, and sends me a link to the campervan. She's obviously been researching this idea for some time, because—as I subsequently learn—many rental companies do not allow dogs.

I open the link and see a shiny red campervan (aka "van"). I've never seen a red quite like this red! It looks spacious, too. I swipe through photos of the van, seeing the large kitchenette, the sleeping area (it sleeps four), and the side awning that can be propped up to create a shaded patio. J is so excited about the van! We were planning on using the Jeep in conjunction with camping tents, meaning she would be sleeping in one tent with the dogs and I'd be in another. I guess the idea of sleeping outside under the stars wasn't terribly appealing, so she did her homework and found a way to be comfortable *and* outdoors at the same time.

I'm quickly processing all of this. Seeing as it costs $250 per day, it's going to double our expenses, for one thing. That's my initial concern, but I'm also concerned about the whole idea of not being true to the outdoors. The point of a camping and hiking trip is that you *don't* have certain amenities—that's part of "being one with nature." This campervan plan puts a fork into that. I'm getting bummed already! But I don't give her my usual immediate "no"—instead, I say, "Let me think about it, and I'll get back to you."

After hanging up, I give this some serious thought. Maybe ten days of "roughing it" would be too much for her, I concede. *With the van, the dogs will have somewhere to stay while we're out and about, we'll have a kitchen with a fridge and stovetop, and lots more storage room. Maybe there's something to be said for that. Plus, she can sleep in the campervan with the dogs, and I'll still have my tent, which is good—having separate spaces is the key to good harmony while traveling no matter whom you're with and where you're going. Yes, this may actually work...*

I call her back with a "yes." She's thrilled! She's making the reservation right now, she tells me. Wow! The trip is now turning into a real adventure. J has definitely done some homework (not surprising). She's been all over YouTube and is sending me links to sites about campervan travelers. Turns out it's a really big thing out in the travel world... Huh! Who knew!

Time to get back to meal planning. Armed with the new information that we'll have a refrigerator and a stovetop the whole time, I can now actually shop for the entire trip. I'm looking up recipes for vegetarian dishes. Hmm... Mexican cuisine ranks high in terms of the possibilities it offers: breakfast tacos, lunch tacos, guacamole, quesadillas. And we both love Mexican food.

———————

Every single day for days and days, I keep checking the Yosemite camping grounds website… and one day out of nowhere, four consecutive days open up during the exact days of our Yosemite schedule! I can't believe it. For a full minute, I keep staring at the laptop screen, but then I shake myself into motion and run to the bedroom to grab my credit card. I type in my information and stare very hard at the dates to confirm that yes, this is real, and I see that yes, it is. I hit the Submit button and receive a confirmation. I've got it!! Four days/nights reserved at Upper Pines in Yosemite National Park.

I'm doing a dance because I'm so incredibly happy. Joy is oozing out of my pores just thinking about the road trip and visiting Yosemite and going hiking and summiting Half Dome! Hallelujah! What unreal luck—we're only two weeks out, and I got us a campsite reservation.

I text J, "We've got our camping site!" Now the only thing left to do on my end is to get the permit to hike Half Dome. I'm hoping I'll get just as lucky with that, but I won't be able to apply til we're at Yosemite—it's a forty-eight-hour window to the proposed date. J texts back, "Hurray!" She's diligently working on nailing down the spa reservations, the wine tastings and the campsite reservations in Napa Valley and Big Sur.

My anticipation is rising, and I know hers is, too. That's what road trips and travel do for the psyche: create great excitement and a renewed zest for discovery.

Chapter 7

Kojak

T'S NOW THE week of our trip, and lots of final prepa-
rations are under way: I've completed a rough daily
menu of our meals and shopped at grocery stores
and farmers markets for our ingredients, and I've laid
out what I'll pack for each part of the trip (the most
important being my hiking gear). According to the
weather report, it'll be the coolest at Yosemite, where
the temps will be in the fifties during the day and in
the thirties and forties at night. I'm bringing lots of
layers: warm knit caps, scarves, gloves, heavy socks, a
fleece jacket, rainwear; and hiking boots, hiking poles,
a headlamp and a water bladder.

I email J a checklist of everything I'm packing so
that she'll have a good starting reference for what to
bring. She's finalized reservations at camping sites at
Napa Valley and Big Sur (which should be beautiful!),

and I'm beginning to look forward to that second half of the trip as well, even though my main focus remains Yosemite.

She's preparing everything for the dogs, too: their food, vitamins, treats, beds, blankets, toys and hiking coats. She's also bringing a large doggie crate for Striker. Where exactly is that going to fit? I have no idea. But we'll figure it out once we get the van and start to pack.

A couple of days before we embark on our trip, she sends me a short text with a link to the campervan video. Good idea! This way, we can get acquainted with the essential van operations prior to our departure. I open the link to the video and start watching. A few minutes into it, I text, "Are you kidding?? I'm going to shoot you." This thing looks complicated at first view! I've never been in an RV or a campervan (and neither has she), so none of this looks familiar. The van has three sources of energy: propane, electrical and battery. The refrigerator must always be running off of the battery unless the van is running. What? I'm going to need to review this video multiple times, I can tell. Then there are the black and gray water tank disposals. *What??* We've got to deal with *toilet water??* When you look at a decked-out RV or a renovated Airstream and see how cool they look, you never really think about all the behind-the-scenes intricacies like power sources or where does the water go or how does the water get out… But these are all good questions.

This requires a full-throttle, time-sucking review, and I'm in no mood to do that—there are too many other things to think about and do right now. We've only got a couple of days until we depart, after all. So I text her back, "Hey, your idea, so please make sure you've got it covered."

"Ha, ha," she texts back. "We've got this."

Here we go! Stress is already creeping in. I just wanted a simple camping trip, but now I've got to spend hours reviewing and re-reviewing how to dispose of gray and black water, which energy source to use when, and how to roll up and down the awning… and the audio system, too. A road trip isn't a road trip without music!

T-minus two days until our trip. J texts and says she needs some new hiking boots and a backpack. This is because she's never *had* hiking boots or a backpack. Where should she go? she asks. I recommend REI.

To repeat, this is the *day prior* to us picking up the van and packing our gear. She's just *now* buying boots and a backpack. I'm getting text after text from her (while she's shopping) with photos of various colors and styles of boots and backpacks. I stress that it's not about style but more about quality of wear. She needs to buy good equipment, not haute couture equipment. She lands on a pink-and-purple Patagonia backpack (which is so her style) and good hiking boots. When I ask her if she has any hiking pants, she says she's taking yoga pants. "Oh, dear God, no! Yoga pants are not for hiking! Buy a pair of hiking pants," I text her.

J loves strong, vibrant colors—her wardrobe is a kaleidoscope of purple and pink hues. I, on the other hand, am into darker tones like black, navy and shades of gray. I think that's because back in the day, outdoor gear manufacturers like Patagonia and The North Face mainly offered those colors. That color palette has definitely changed since (thank goodness), but over the years, I've acquired a lot of outdoor clothing, and I'm not buying anything new.

Because we're headed north, the plan is for me to drive up to Los Angeles tomorrow. We'll pick up the campervan together, take it back to J's house, load everything and get started early the next day. It's approximately a six-hour drive to Yosemite, including making one stop to get coffee and gas and let the dogs out for a bit.

The following day, I lock up my house, leave Laguna Beach in mid-afternoon and arrive at J's by 3 p.m. The back of my Jeep is filled with backpacks, the tent, lamps, my sleeping bag, hiking poles, my yoga mat (yes, I have one, too; I use it as a sleeping mat) and lots of food that we'll be storing in the refrigerator. I arrive at J's house and am met by the dogs, who are both happy. They know something special is happening! Striker's tail is fervently wagging and Stormy is actually going around the house smelling all of the bags and items that are staged for loading at the front of the house. I love it that the dogs are feeling what we're feeling…

J's not quite done with her packing, but she wants to show me all of her new outfits. They're all cute, indeed…but she's still packing her things, and we need to go pick up the campervan in the San Fernando Valley, which is an hour's drive away. We decide I'll drive my Jeep and leave it there. J suggests we take the dogs for the ride. My immediate "no" kicks in this time—we don't need any distractions while we're being schooled on the van and its operations. Thankfully, she agrees.

Driving from Hwy 405 North to Hwy 101 North, we're now in what's termed "the valley." I exit the 101, and after a few turns, I drive up to a gate in the middle of a dusty equestrian property. When I ask the guard for Andy, we're directed to follow a long driveway filled with horse manure that leads to a small building at the back of the property. I try to avoid driving through the piles of poop, but that's an impossible task. I'm not sure what I expected, but this wasn't it. J has been coordinating all of the reservations and has had conversations with Andy; I've left all of this up to her. I had assumed we'd be going to a car rental type of establishment, not a horse farm.

As we near the small building that looks more like stalls than an office, we see a very, very red van. We look at each other and start to laugh. This has to be our van! Yes, there it is…as we get closer, we see "Kojak" written on the side of it. That's what we'd seen in the website photos, too. We have found our transportation.

Andy is a nice bohemian 50-something outdoorsy type of guy who's traveled all over the U.S. with the campervan. He owns two German shepherds who are well-behaved and sitting by the steps of the van. I'm so glad we didn't bring J's dogs.

His quick story to us is that he bought a van and had it converted into a campervan. He uses it a few months out of the year to go on long road trips to national parks and then rents it out for the rest of the year to have some additional income. There are apps and websites that now assist owners who have personal RV/campervan vehicles to rent, just like an Airbnb lodging. Few owners allow pets, but he does since he clearly has a strong appreciation for bringing pets along on a road trip. I can tell by the way he looks at his dogs that he treasures that experience.

He starts to give us the tour. At the front of the van, there are two swivel seats: a driver's seat and a passenger seat split by a huge mid-section storage divider. Behind the driver's seat is a dining area for four people, complete with a table that folds down. This entire area turns itself into a bed that sleeps two. When you slide the campervan door open on the passenger side, this is the area you see first. What's nice is there's a screen door, so we'll be able to keep the door open and enjoy being al fresco yet insect-free while we're at campsites. This area also houses the monitor for the power sources and the audio system, and there's lots of overhead storage. Behind the dining area is the kitchenette, complete with a nice-size refrigerator, a stovetop oven, a microwave, a kitchen sink and more storage space. Finally, at the back sits the bathroom, which has a toilet, sink and open shower (with a hand-held sprayer). There's more storage space above and a pull-down, full-size bed. What's really nice about this set-up is that behind the rear doors of the van, Andy has added a storage carriage, providing lots more storage space without taking up any more interior space.

J is paying close attention, I see. Hopefully that means she's got it. I'm standing nearby, half-listening and mostly nodding. He points to the power sources and emphasizes that this is the Very Important Part of the Tour. Now I start to really focus on what he's showing us. There's the battery, which is powered when the van is running; there's the electrical hook-up that you use when you park and attach the long cord to an electrical outlet at the campsite; and then there's the built-in generator that's powered by the horrible-fume-emitting propane tanks. At times, each energy source should be used for specific appliances, especially the refrigerator, Andy explains.

Okay, think I've got it, and J definitely has it. We're good here. Now comes the emptying of the tanks. Yuck! Now we get to learn about gray water (wastewater that drains from the kitchen and shower) and black water (wastewater that drains from the toilet). J is asking a bunch of good questions. There are latex gloves in a small box attached to the outside of the van. I'm not going there. She has this.

Finally, we get to the awning, which requires two people to operate. This was the one (and only) part of the video I did actually watch. While Andy looks on, J and I practice rolling the awning up and then down. We get it in one try! I'm so proud of us! We shimmy into a high-five.

He hands the keys to J… and she quickly hands them to me and asks, "Do you want to drive?"

What?? I think. *This is your baby! Don't you want to try it first?* Clearly, she does not, though, so okay, I'll drive. I get in the driver's seat.

Andy says, "It handles really well—it just requires wide turns." I mention that I once drove a U-Haul, and he grins. "Perfect!" he says. "This is just like that." I glance over at J and see that she's grinning, too.

I shake my head at her. *I'm beginning to think I've just been selected as the designated driver…*

We head back to J's house and park the very red campervan in her driveway. We prop the doors open and start loading the van with our backpacks, suitcases, food, drinks, lots of wine… Basically, everything we'll need is stored in the refrigerator and interior storage bins. The outside storage carrier is filled with the big heavy bag of dog food, treats and bowls, and we also utilize that space for my tent, sleeping bag, lamps, yoga mats and hiking poles.

It seems we're creating a bit of a commotion, because neighbors walking by J's house start to approach us to see what's going on. "Wow!" they say. "That's a pretty cool van!" Everyone wants to take a peek inside. Judging from everyone's reactions, it's pretty obvious we will be noticed on the road and in the campsites. Striker and Stormy come out and jump into the van to see what all the fuss is about and to get a glimpse of what will be their new home for the next ten days. They really like it, I can tell.

As the dogs acclimate themselves to their new surroundings, jumping up and down the front seats, swiveling round and round, J and I feast on a gluten-free pizza and a bottle of wine at the dining table. This will be our one and only time at the dining table.

Meanwhile, more and more neighbors continue to stroll by and peer in.

Chapter 8

Coffee

NEXT MORNING, WE'RE up early and on the road at 7 a.m. I'm driving, J's in the passenger seat and the two dogs are in the back, Striker in his crate on the floor below the pull-down bed and Stormy up on the seat behind the driver's side. We decide (really, J decided last night) to keep the dining table permanently down to make this a little sofa area for Stormy, who claimed it his late last night.

Striker's crate is a beauty! I mean, it's big—it takes up nearly one-third of the floor space. We'll need to climb over the crate to reach the toilet and shower area. When she brought that thing out from the house, I said, "Are you seriously trying to fit that crate in there?" But she was determined to fit it in, and she did. The reason she was so adamant is that not only does Striker like to sleep in the crate, the dogs have had their little scuffles at times, and having Striker in his crate is how she likes to separate them. But the quarters are really tight back there! Nonetheless, it's her space, and I'm just going with the flow at this stage.

As we loaded our last-minute items into the van this morning, both dogs had a "We're going somewhere!" enthusiasm about them. Sensing something adventurous was occurring, they kept following us in and out of the house. The very last thing we had to get into the van were the dogs, which wasn't easy—Striker's cone-wrapped head was banging against almost everything in his way, including Stormy. His front right leg was still completely bandaged, so he had to hop along until J finally placed him gingerly in his crate. He seems like he's getting stronger, but he's still very much emotionally dependent on J and doesn't want to be separated from her at all. Stormy has taken to all the activity with a new-found sense of vitality. The dining-area-turned-sofa-area seems to be quite to his liking. This would have been my area if I had wanted to sleep in the van, but I've relinquished this space to Stormy because my tent will hold my solace, outside within nature and underneath the stars.

The van feels pretty good to drive—it does handle well, and I can make the turns without any problems. It's nice and high, too, so I have visibility far in front of me, much better than what I'd get with any SUV. I'm so relieved that the van is turning out to be a good idea!

It's a sunny and cool fifty-degree morning in LA as we head north on Hwy 405 North, then Hwy 5 North and finally CA 99, where we'll be for most of this drive. J and I are in that road-trip, adventure-happy mood—you know, that feeling you get when you've been planning a trip for weeks and the day has finally come. It's the greatest feeling when the journey finally starts!

We are getting some long stares on the highway from other drivers as they pass us, probably because of the very red color of the van. It's a strong color, to put it mildly. We smile and nod back as if to say, "Yes, we know." Sometimes we actually do say that out loud at the same time, looking at each other and laughing/giggling. We're on our way… What a glorious feeling!

A couple of hours into the drive, we reach Bakersfield and decide to top off the gas tank and grab some coffee. It'll be my first one for the day, and I'm very much in need of it. We exit off the CA 99 and see a coffee shop next to a gas station. Perfect! We begin the process of moving the dogs out of the van. Yes, I said "process," because it most certainly is one. As usual, I take Stormy and J has Striker. We have the collars, leashes and poop bags for both dogs, plus treats for Stormy in case we need to entice him to move. The van has a step-down, which greatly assists us with both Striker and Stormy given their injury and ailments. J opens up the crate and gets Striker's collar and leash on as he's frantically moving towards the door. He badly wants out. He proceeds to jump completely out of the van without the help of the step and immediately starts to throw up green funky slime.

What the…? I'm *so* thankful he waited until he got out of the van! That's my kind of dog. Stormy looks over and just continues to do his own thing. As J is caring for poor Striker, I can only stare in disbelief. She's frowning, clearly worried. "He's been fine!" she says. "I don't understand why he's throwing up his food."

I get carsick sometimes, so I wonder if he might have the same problem. "Maybe being on the floor in the crate is giving him motion sickness?" I suggest. He does look a little green in the eyes. J can only shrug helplessly.

We walk the dogs around the parking lot for about ten minutes. Striker is looking a little better—there's some life coming back into his eyes, and his tail is up again wagging a somewhat happy wag. Hopefully he just needed some air. We both agree that he probably just got carsick. J says she's going to keep him outside of the crate on these long hauls and see if he and Stormy can sit on the sofa area together without any territorial issues. I think, *not likely.*

We get the dogs back into the van without too much trouble. They both hop onto the sofa behind me (designated as "Stormy's spot"), and almost immediately, Stormy doesn't agree to the new shared seating arrangement even though there's plenty of space for both dogs. I hear growling. *This must be what it's like to have kids, right?* I think. I can tell that J's feeling anxious about how the two dogs are going to get along back there.

She goes to the back of the van where the full-size bed is stored, pulls it down and takes Striker to it. He happily jumps onto it and lies down still with his cone on, his sweet eyes still popping out a little green. A new peace seems to have been established—we now all have our spaces, especially the dogs. Big sigh! Time to get moving… except that I haven't had my coffee yet.

That's not a good thing—by 10 a.m., I need my almond milk latte with its shots of espresso. Just that one cup! I stress to J, "I need coffee," and she knows what that means.

She nods in understanding. "Let's go!" she says, and I drive us to the coffee shop. Unfortunately, when I attempt to go through the drive-thru, I can't make it—the height of the campervan doesn't allow for it. I must back up and get out of the drive-thru lane and into the parking lot. That's not going to be so easy, though, because there is a line of cars behind me. Ugh! *Does it have to be this complicated,* I think. J steps out and directs everybody to back up. This causes Striker to jump out of the bed and Stormy to jump out of the sofa. They're both barking "like mad" as they watch through the side windows their mommy directing traffic. I look behind my chair and beg them both to calm down.

I'm beginning to realize that almost nothing on this trip is going to be easy. Nothing. Even getting a cup of coffee is going to take more effort! Once I've got my coffee in hand, I'll be better able to accept this realization. I park and go in to retrieve our morning drinks. I've finally, finally got my coffee!

I jump into the driver's seat and start sipping the latte. A beautiful calmness settles in—I'm feeling better, a lot better. J is, too. Just as importantly (more importantly?), the dogs have settled in and are being quiet. Next, I drive over to the gas station and am able to fill the gas tank without any drama. Just more stares at the campervan, which I'm now pretty accustomed to and have created (an impressive) "nod and smile" response for.

Things are good. We're back on CA 99, heading north. Now all that's missing are some good tunes. Oh, no! I was going to put together a playlist specifically for this road trip. So much to do that I totally forgot. I'll do that later tonight or tomorrow when I'm quietly in my tent, I decide. In the meantime, we've got old-school radio.

J is in charge of music and navigation. This is not expressed but implied since I'm driving. After about fifteen minutes of music, she asks if she can put on a yoga podcast or some other type of well-being podcast she's been listening to. I almost cringe at the thought, but the music wasn't that great, so I say, "Okay." She puts it on. It's that woman again, the one with the horribly high-pitched voice. After about five minutes, my head is exploding. *Please, no. What is she talking about??*

I look over at J. She asks, "Is this good?"

I'm sure she can see the pained expression on my face. "Not really."

"Okay, then, let's turn it off."

"Great!" I say. *Thank you,* I think. We just keep listening to an Eighties rock-and-roll station for a while—that works fine for both of us.

The scenery along this route is downright uninteresting, but we're stuck with it. During springtime, snow is a major problem in the upper elevations, and although going through Tioga Pass at the east end of the Sierra Mountains would have been the most scenic route, we didn't have that option since Hwy 120 is closed during this season. Soon, we'll be leaving CA 99 and taking internal Hwy Route 41 into Yosemite National Park. Before we get to the park entrance, though, we stop to pick up some firewood for the campfire. Everyone but J stays in the van as she goes into the small market and purchases the firewood. (J has been designated by me as owning the campfires while I prepare our evening dinners.) While J's in the market, the dogs have remained in their places with little commotion—*good,* I think.

She throws the firewood in the rear outside carriage

and we re-begin our journey towards Yosemite. We're not far now. But, it's all two-lane roads from here—a slow drive. We're passing through small towns, in the heart of California's gold country. Now we're heading onto Route 41 and starting to climb in elevation. We're near the south park entrance just past Wawona when we start to see a backup of cars. "We're almost at the entrance!" I yell.

J and I high-five, our huge smiles beaming. It's slow going here, but pretty soon, we see the sign for Yosemite National Park. Traffic is moving at a snail's pace, so we quickly get out of the van (before the dogs have a chance to jump out after us) to take a couple of selfies in front of the park sign. Most of the other people waiting in their cars to get into the park are doing the same thing.

At the ranger's station, we pay our entrance fee and start to drive through the park. We're really climbing in elevation—we're up to almost 4,000 feet. Wow! J's checking in the back to see if Striker and Stormy are okay. The roads are slowly winding. It's quite a lovely drive, the anticipation of entering the Lower Valley is palpable.

We finally reach the long, dark Wawona Tunnel. After driving for a half-mile in the tunnel, we exit out the other side, and without any warning, a majestic view of granite walls spreads out in front of us and gives me a nearly indescribable feeling. "Yosemite!"

I scream out. Far away in the distance, I can see El Capitan, Half Dome and Bridalveil Fall. "Holy Moly!" I scream out again. "Wow!"

Immediately upon exiting the tunnel, there's a viewing area to the left. I quickly pull into it. We are all so happy to be in the park—I'm bouncing up and down in my seat. "We're here, we're here!" and the dogs are up and excited and ready to get out. Per practice, J and I quickly assemble all of the doggie accessories and clip on their leashes before we slide the campervan door open. Each dog leaps out as if they're in Doggie Disneyland. They're not even waiting for the step-down to come out. They are electrified—they've never seen nor smelled anything like this before! Holding them back is a challenge, especially with Striker, who's completely lost his doggie mind. Their noses are awash with the "(Lower) Yosemite Valley" smells and their ears keep twitching with every noise. They can sense they have arrived at nature's gate.

Chapter 9

Tunnel View

THIS IS AN extraordinary sight! No words could possibly describe what I'm feeling as we look out on a panoramic view of enormous slabs of granite rocks jutting up from a spectacular valley. There they are: El Capitan, Half Dome and Bridalveil Fall, all nestled into the stunningly beautiful Lower Yosemite Valley. I'm just staring, completely in awe of nature. For a brief moment, electricity fills my veins and tears fill my eyes. Given all I've read and seen online, I just knew it would be gorgeous, but this is more than I expected.

Yosemite Valley is a glacial valley with a number of streams and rivers draining through it, including the Merced River. El Capitan is a sheer granite face—the largest in the world, actually—that rises 3,000 feet tall. For experienced rock climbers, this is a mecca, one of the holy grails. (I recently saw the documentary *Free Solo* about Alex Honnold, who climbed El Capitan free solo, meaning he didn't use any ropes or equipment. He's an amazing athlete and my hero in every sense of the word!) Then there's Half Dome. It's at an elevation of 4,700 feet and sits in the center and back of this view. It's another granite rock formation, but its three sides are smooth and round, making it look like a dome that's been cut in half. For avid hikers like me, Half Dome is definitely on the bucket list. I hope to be on the summit of Half Dome in just a few days. (Fingers crossed I'm able to secure a lottery permit.) Finally, Bridalveil Fall is on the right of my current vantage point, jutting upwards approximately 600 feet with its waters flowing into Yosemite Valley, which is home to sprawling meadows and a dense forest of pine trees. I've had the privilege of seeing many extraordinary parks all around the world, but this view is up there with the best of them.

Although there are others around me—tourists, professional and amateur photographers, Stormy, J and Striker—I've tuned everyone out and I continue staring at the view, soaking it in. This is what I came to experience! This, what I'm feeling *right now*. I feel so blessed and fortunate, blessed and happy to be in this moment.

After ten minutes, I look around amongst all the tourists and spot J, who's struggling to keep Striker under control. With a skip in my step, I walk over with Stormy at my side and a childlike beam on my face. "Isn't it something??" I shout.

She's apparently too preoccupied with Striker's fixation on a squirrel to really take it all in. "Yeah, it's great," she says (with not much enthusiasm), as she pulls on Striker's leash. I don't think she's had much of a chance to absorb what we're in the middle of— Striker is still attempting to run after a squirrel, in the process hurdling over the two-foot-tall stone wall in front of us. But for the wall and J's leash, we would never see him again. The animal life below is proving too much for him to remain composed and calm.

Stormy, on the other hand, has been discovered by some Japanese tourists who clearly adore him and are asking for permission from me to take pictures with him. He's now become a photo prop, and he's milking the attention. It's astounding to see his renewed sense of energy—he's so electrified after a six-and-a-half-hour van ride! It's heartening to see how these dogs have transformed themselves given their respective age- and injury-related ailments.

J and I take lots of photos of ourselves in front of the expansive views of what many describe as a "temple of nature." Photographers with their tripods are lined up here at the short wall and across the road above to get shots of the iconic landmarks in the background and the Lower Yosemite Valley in the foreground. It's fascinating to talk to the professional photographers and look into their lenses—factors like the time of day, the seasons, the clouds and the angle of the sunlight all alter the granite monuments' light in the photos. We arrived just past midday, and the sun is slipping in and out of the roaming clouds above, presenting us an array of photo opportunities.

We finish taking pictures and videos, including posting some on Instagram (surprisingly, there's cell service at this spot), and then begin the very last part of today's road trip: driving through the Lower Valley and finding the campsite that will be our home for the next four nights.

———————

It's late afternoon now, and we are all tired and hungry. We're also relieved that we've arrived. Finally! We're actually here at Yosemite National Park, at our campsite #84 in the Upper Pines. Pinch me! The campsites are rather tight, with each one abutting the next, but that's okay—the location is amazing. We're in the middle of the valley floor filled with towering pine trees, and the Merced River is only a few hundred yards away. The small paved road running along the riverbanks, filled with bicyclists right now, will be perfect for dog walks. Now I wish we had brought our bikes.

We're a few hours away from sunset, and the campground is full of RVs and tents. I back up the campervan in between the logs that designate our campsite. We have enough space on the right side to roll out our awning and lay out the rattan rug, but first things first! We open the side door and let the dogs out, then tie them to the picnic table as we begin to unload and set up camp. Given all the excitement at Tunnel View, the dogs are much more relaxed now—J throws down their doggie beds and, thankfully, both have plopped themselves down and are quietly observing their new environment, watching J and I move things out of the rear carriage storage bin.

An initial quick glance shows that our campsite neighbors to the right and left have yet to arrive, though our neighbors behind us have a very nice RV with quite an elaborate outdoor set-up, including tables, chairs, dining and lounge tents, table linens, dinnerware and stemware. I see two people and go over to say hello and introduce myself and J. They're a nice couple from Encino, California, and this is their fifth visit to Yosemite. They have bikes and kayaks and mention they're here for the entire week. I'm so jealous.

Before I start making dinner, I begin setting up my blue tent to the right of the campervan. Wireframe technology has made set-up so easy these days! It only takes five minutes to get it all up. It's a sweet little two-person tent and looks adorable (if I do say so myself) next to the campervan. The dogs are now curious about what I'm doing and are trying to pull themselves over to me, but fortunately, their leashes are keeping them confined to the picnic table area. I transfer my sleeping bag and yoga mat from the rear carriage to the tent and add some throws and my backpack. My little "tent home" feels cozy.

In the meantime, J has pulled out the twenty-pound bag of dog food and all of their vitamins and treats and placed them in the bear locker at the back of our campsite. At the ranger's station, we received a quick two-minute tutorial on how to store our food, but seeing as we have a refrigerator, the only thing we have to worry about storing is the dog food.

Next, J pulls out the blue camping chairs and blue rattan rug and unfolds the red-and-white tablecloth. Not only does our space look like a red-white-and-blue patriotic zone, it looks amazingly cute, too. (We hadn't planned the patriotic part, but it has certainly come together.) Some final touches include rolling up the awning and laying out J's red yoga mat. Neighbors are taking notice as they walk by, and we "nod and smile" and then look at each other and laugh. The color red sure does attract people!

After using the camp restrooms and taking a quick stroll around the grounds, it's time to start dinner. We're having cheese quesadillas and guacamole with chips. When J asks if she can help, I say, "Yes—you can open up a bottle of wine." She pours us glasses, and we say "Cheers!" and take our first sip in the kitchen area. J's not much help in the kitchen, though, so she heads outside and starts figuring out how to start a fire. I think this may be her first campfire… Soon, I hear her chatting with the neighbors. That's another good thing about J—she'll either figure it out or find someone who can help her figure things out.

I'm starting with the guacamole. When I cut open the avocados, they are picture-worthy gorgeous and just ripe enough. I smash the avocado flesh in a bowl and add some lime juice along with small bits of jalapeño, tomatoes, red onions and garlic. Yum! Along with some fresh corn chips bought at my farmers market last weekend, we are ready to start dinner.

But before we put everything on the picnic table, J wants to feed the dogs first—that will avoid chaos as we eat, she says. Even though I'm starving, I have to agree with her logic. As I put the finishing touches on the guacamole, J gets out the big bag of dog food and two bowls. The dogs devour their food in less than thirty seconds. That was fast!

It's now sunset. J has gotten a fire going, and it looks great. I've brought out the guacamole and chips, and we finally sit down on the picnic table with our bottle of wine. We share a big, big sigh. This is so awesome! It's been a long day, but a great day. The guacamole is delicious, and we linger over it as we share some laughs about our day. By now, I'm so tired that I can't muster up the energy to make the quesadillas I had said I'd make. I ask if cheese and crackers will be okay for dinner instead. "Sure!" she says. Good thing she's not a picky eater.

First, though, she recommends that we take the dogs for their evening walk. What can I say? I'm exhausted at this point, but we do have dogs with us, and they need to be walked. Unbelievably, they've picked up quite a bit of energy during their little respite, so we need to make sure they're tired enough to go to sleep soon. We get out our dog accessories and go for a walkabout around the campsite.

The aromas of everyone's dinners are on full display at this point in the evening. Some people are grilling, giving us a hint of hamburgers and hotdogs; some are sautéing onions and peppers on their camp stoves; others have elaborate set-ups within their RVs and Airstreams, and we catch the occasional glimpse of them preparing large meals in their kitchens. *Jeez, all I've made for us is guacamole*, I think. *Yes, it was really good and made with fresh, organic ingredients, but I need to step it up tomorrow.*

The dogs' level of excitement has only slightly diminished from earlier in the day—they're walking around and smelling every tree, rock and plant they encounter, Striker hopping along on his three-and-a-half legs and Stormy pulling me along and leading all of us despite his age. What nature does to dogs is unmatched!

We've walked around for about forty-five minutes, and it's now dark. Even with our headlamps, still, it's hard to find our campsite. Finally, we make out a red campervan in the distance. How fortunate that our "home" stands out so well! The fact that we're the only red vehicle within the campgrounds makes it easy to find.

Back at the campsite, J adds a few more logs to the fire. I think she's got a good handle on it. With the dogs once again tied to the picnic table, I bring out the cheeseboard and crackers. It may not be a real dinner, but the various organic cheeses are quite good, and the wine makes it all delicious.

As I start to clean up, J puts out the fire with a little water. By this hour, the dogs are ready to call it a night. Before J takes them both into the van, she asks if I want Stormy with me in the tent. I say "Ummm…" and stall for a second, but I know that she knows the answer to that. "No, thanks," I finally say. "I think he'll be much more comfortable in the van with you. And I'll be more comfortable, too." She just laughs in response.

Striker jumps into the van and into his crate, Stormy settles himself on the sofa, J gets into bed and I crawl into my tent. It's been a long day. I can't wait for tomorrow's hike around the Lower Valley!

Chapter 10

Hiking With Dogs

THE TENT IS my comfort spot and my Zen zone. It's where I can deliberate, meditate and reflect on my day and how I feel. Am I nurturing my soul? Am I present? Am I happy and am I feeling at peace internally? I can think about all of these things within my cheerful space. The throws and blankets I added to my interior have made the tent quite restful. When I lay down and look up, I'm filled with a sense of peacefulness, self-love and blessedness.

The temperature tonight will hover in the low forties, making it pretty chilly, so I've thrown on about five layers, including a thermal base, knit cap, scarf and gloves. I also have an excellent goose down sleeping bag from years of camping in colder temperatures. I'm not cold at all—I feel really comfortable, actually. Fatigue sets in as soon as I lay down, and I fall asleep immediately.

In the middle of the night, I wake up needing to use the bathroom. Oh, my God, I hate leaving my tent in the middle of the night! I'm a bit spooked by animals that might be nearby, especially bears—I've heard and read a lot about the bear population entering campgrounds more and more these days. But I can't hold it, so I unzip my sleeping bag, turn on my headlamp, pick up the big stick I brought into the tent with me, pick up my phone (don't know why—who am I going to call?—and there's no service in the park, anyway) and put my flip-flops on over my socks. It's pitch-dark as I unzip the tent fly, but luckily, the dim light coming from the surrounding RV campers does provide some visibility. I reflexively look up in search of stars and don't see many. I guess we're not high enough and surrounded by too many tall pine trees. Stargazing would be another fun activity, but that will be for another trip.

The toilets are only one hundred yards away. I make a very quick dash and complete my business, wash my hands in the freezing sink water and walk briskly back to the tent. Deep breath…I made it!

I check my phone and see that it's 3 a.m. I can't get back to sleep—I'm wide awake and am starting to hear noises. Are they coming from animals or people? I listen intently, trying to tell what's making those sounds. I do this for three hours. By 6 a.m., Stormy is typically up and ready for his walk, so I unzip the tent and head over to the campervan. When I slide open the door, I see Stormy lying awake on the sofa. He's happy to see me—he jumps up and wants to rush to me, but I hold him back until I've pulled the step down so that he won't hurt himself. I see J in the back of the van. She's still asleep, I assume. I think Striker is, too, but it's too dark to see the crate. He must be asleep, though, because he isn't making any noises, even though the sun has risen and it's daylight. It's just me and Stormy taking our first morning walk together. How nice.

As we walk through the campgrounds, Stormy is pulling his leash and once more smelling every plant, every bush, every tree prior to squatting and doing his thing. He's clearly enjoying everything the pine forest has to offer. We walk about a quarter of a mile along the Merced River and cross the Sentinel Bridge. What a view Half Dome is at sunrise! It's hard to tell who's happier, me or Stormy. During this time of year (May), the river is flowing with snow melt and making a gentle, soothing sound.

Stormy and I keep walking, heading to Half Dome Village. It's about a mile away, and it's also where there's Wi-Fi and I'll be able to apply for the coveted daily Half Dome hiking permit. It's where the coffee shop is, too, and I'm ready for my cup! The Village is below Half Dome and Glacier Point, and its location makes it quite a sight. We pass a row of cabins and are met by other dog walkers along the paved road and walking trails. What a morning! The smells of the trees—pine, oak, sequoia, cedar—are extraordinary. Stormy has a special kick to his step and is really relishing our surroundings.

As we walk, the daylight becomes more pronounced; by the time we get there, it's downright sunny. I can't take Stormy inside, so I tie his leash to one of the benches outside. It's still early and not many people are around—getting a coffee shouldn't take long. Only a couple of people are ahead of me in line. I order my coffee and am back outside with a cup of water for Stormy while they make my latte. He must be thirsty, because he gulps his water, getting slobber everywhere on his face. A few parents and children come up asking to pet him. He's really good with strangers, especially children.

I get my latte and sit on the wooden bench next to Stormy and submit my online application for the Half Dome permit. I'm looking up at the sky when I hit the Submit button. *Here's praying I get selected!* For now, though, it's time to return to the campsite.

At this hour, campers are starting to rise. I smell breakfasts being made and see more dog walkers and hikers wearing their puffed jackets and knit caps, taking strolls. The air is still quite cool. I exchange lots of "Good mornings" on the way back and get general "Ahhs" as people see Stormy, who has that "old grandpa" dog look: gentle and sweet.

As I turn the corner and head to our campsite, I can see Striker tied to the picnic table and J practicing her morning yoga next to him. She tells me she has just come back from walking Striker, who apparently got too close to a coyote. She didn't sleep well, either, she says—it was too cold, and because the official "quiet hours" in the park begin at 10 p.m. and go on until 6 a.m., she couldn't run the generator to turn on the heat, so she pulled Striker out of his crate and onto her bed and they spooned last night.

Speaking of the dogs, it's time for their breakfast. She starts their meal routine, dragging out the dog food bags, bowls and vitamins from the bear locker. I go into the campervan and pull out the carafe of almond milk and a box of granola. It's nothing fancy—just a light breakfast—but it's good to put a little something in my belly prior to our hike. She's already had her special coffee (which she made with her coffee machine that she brought from home) plus a banana and yogurt. We're all good on the food front, at least for now. Everyone's happy, everyone's got something in their stomachs and everyone's ready for our first full day of hiking!

We're taking the dogs on the hiking trails that allow pets on leashes. There aren't many, but given Striker's injuries and Stormy's age, we'll have plenty of options—Lower Yosemite Fall and Mirror Lake are pet-friendly trails that are relatively short. Still, it does require a lot of planning to get all of the dogs' gear ready. In addition to the standard items, we're taking lots of additional water, inflatable drinking bowls and a first-aid kit, including extra bandages for Striker. It's only about fifty degrees right now; the weather (and we) will definitely warm up as the day goes on, so as customary, J and I are layering our clothes.

We lock up the campervan and head out. Starting along the Merced River, we walk along a gentle, flat trail that's not too crowded given the time of year. Stormy and I are leading—he's got a heck of a swift doggie pace! Behind us, Striker closes in on everything, at least as much as what J will allow. He's hopping along with long strides on his three good legs and dragging the fourth, his tail wagging with resolve. He's going to capture as much of this environment as is doggie-possible.

As other hikers near towards us, their eyes are drawn to both dogs, and when they see Striker, their eyes widen. "Is he okay?" they want to know. J explains the story, telling them that yes, he broke his leg jumping out of her second-story balcony and that he's had surgery and that he's been through a lot. Our fellow hikers have shocked looks on their faces when they hear about his Super Dog leap. "But he's fine now," she assures them. They're amazed and relieved to hear how well he's progressing—his restored good health is obvious in his face and demeanor. We get so many warm and genuine well-wishes! This exact conversation happens many times throughout the day. It becomes so routine, in fact, that J and I start taking turns explaining how it happened, with assurances that he's doing just fine and he's adjusted and all is well.

Both dogs have their sets of admirers as we walk: some love Stormy's gracefully aging presence, while others are drawn to Striker hopping along on three-and-a-half legs with a cone around his neck. They certainly make for an attraction! Meanwhile, J and I just keep moving along and pause every once in a while to chat. After about three miles, we decide to stop on the banks of the river and have a snack.

Earlier, I put together a few bags of dry fruit, nuts and protein bars; now I take them out of my backpack. J pours some water into bowls for Striker and Stormy, both of whom are panting and clearly ready to drink. They both need a break. We take a seat at the end of Lower Yosemite Trail, which runs along the river-bank and is edged by a foot-high stone wall. I can't get enough of the sounds of the river gently flowing in the background. It's simply serene.

I'm taking a moment to admire the scene in front of me. Sometimes you do have to consciously stop and make mental notes of a moment instead of rushing through it. This entire landscape is stunning, not only because of the iconic granite sites of El Capitan, Half

Dome and Glacier Point, but also the interior park filled with meadows, trees, plant life and the river with its glinting waters and soothing sounds.

I hand J a couple of dried fruit pieces and a handful of nuts. I eat some nuts, but just a few. She looks at me with a strange glare—not a mean one, but a sad, desperate-faced one that says, "Is this all?" I typically don't eat much while hiking, though, so I didn't bring along too much food, especially when it's a short five-mile hike like this one. I look in my bag again and see a couple of oranges and a banana.

I hand them all to her. She smiles. "Oh, good!" She's happy to see more food.

"I'm sorry—I do need to alter my eating habits," I say. My bad. I clearly need to make some adjustments here. With J completely on doggie duty, I've got to make sure I have more food for both of us. *Next time, bring more food and more snacks!* I tell myself.

I glance over at the dogs. Striker is playing with J, but Stormy has a look I've come to recognize, the one that says he's not going to move any time soon. *Oh, no!* "Please don't be done," I murmur quietly.

We get up and put on our backpacks. Striker is up and ready, but—surprise—Stormy doesn't move. (Remember, for one thing, he's deaf.) I'm tugging at the leash, at first gently and then with additional force. "Come on, Stormy!" I plead.

Nothing. He's not budging. J and I just look at each other and shout "Yikes!" at the same time. She opens her bag and pulls out his treats and places them in front of him. Nope. And we can't carry him—he's too heavy.

So, we sit back down and wait. We give him ten more minutes and try again… and he miraculously gets up. "Yay!" I yell. J looks as relieved as I feel. Even more miraculously, now he's leading us, walking at that same brisk pace he was maintaining before. That's amazing! I guess that ten-minute rest was all he needed.

After having averted this potential disaster, J and I rethink whether we should keep going to Mirror Lake, another pet-friendly hiking trail. "He looks good," I say. "Let's keep going."

J hesitates before nodding. "Okay," she agrees, "but if he starts to slow down, we should head back right away."

We come across more people along this trail—it's incredibly popular. Lots more stops with similar conversations about Striker's leg, his Super Dog balcony jump, his surgery and assurances of yes, he's fine now. As the well-wishers pass us and continue along the trail, we can still hear their conversations: "Oh, my, what a sweet dog!" "I can't believe he jumped off a balcony!" "He's such a trooper."

When we reach Mirror Lake, the clouds have started to set in, so we don't see the typical reflection of the sun in the lake—which is why it's called Mirror Lake—but the view is splendid nonetheless. We loop around, still stopping to have light conversations with other hikers. Many of them hadn't realized that certain trails allow for pets. I believe we've encouraged a few to come back with their favorite canines.

Stormy and Striker want another break. They're having a good day! That means more water and a few more treats. J eats the remaining orange as I rummage through my bag again and find more trail mix for her. I'm still not hungry and am just drinking water.

We are stunned at how well both dogs are doing, and I can tell that J is in a very happy internal place—she keeps smiling and seems to have an actual glow. *Is this what Yosemite does to you? Do I have a glow, too?* I wonder. This glow is applied by nature; it's nature's effect, nature's way of washing away stress. Any kind of exercise gets your blood flowing, of course, but this is unique. I feel it.

We start to head back to our campsite. Stormy gets to his feet, but his pace has definitely slowed down. He's moving, though, and that's all that matters right now, because the treats bag is dwindling. As we walk out of the Mirror Lake Trail and head back along the paved road, we collectively share a big sigh. We made it! I can't believe how much energy the dogs had in completing both of those trails.

Marked with our red van, our campsite is easily visible from a few hundred yards away. Both dogs are wiped out. When we leash them to the picnic table, they immediately lie down on their doggie beds with happy, tired faces. I think they have their own glows. Doggie glows.

Time for cocktail hour! J opens a bottle of Sauvignon Blanc, pours two glasses and passes one to me. "Cheers to another great day!" we chorus as we gently clink our glasses. I head to the kitchen to start making dinner. Tonight, it will be a bountiful one: tortilla soup and cheese quesadillas piled high.

Chapter 11

Bear

Today J and I will be hiking up Mist Trail to Vernal Fall and Nevada Fall, two very popular and legendary hikes because of the sights and sounds of the waterfalls. It's a seven-mile round trip with an elevation of 1,900 feet. J has made accommodations to leave both dogs at the Yosemite Valley Stable, a nine-stall kennel. The drawback is that the kennel is near horses, and we're not sure how Striker and Stormy will react since this will be a first for them. Hopefully they'll handle it well. This will also be J's first major hike. I'm excited for us to leave the dogs in good hands and really challenge ourselves with an uphill trail! Granted, I'm also a little worried that this may be too much for her, but we'll take things slowly. Besides, when J sets her mind to do something, she's determined.

After a restful night of sleep (no middle-of-the-night bathroom run, no unrecognizable noises), I'm ready. My adrenaline is already flowing as I think about today's hikes and all that we'll see. I get up and out of my tent early and grab Stormy out of the van. We start our morning walk. J and Striker are knocked out, still asleep together on the bed. The campgrounds are quiet and the sun hasn't fully risen yet, making it a lovely time to be out and about. Soon, crowds of campers will start their day.

Stormy starts out strong as we roam the riverbanks. He continues to savor the smells of all of the plant and animal life, squatting and doing his business every few yards even when there's really nothing left. I sense a slight slowing of his pace, though, so we skip the mile-long walk to the coffee shop and instead head back to the campsite, where I'll forego today's coffee and make myself tea instead. I think I can manage without my coffee for one day. I don't want to overextend Stormy given that five-mile hike we all did yesterday, plus I've got to prepare for the bigger hike J and I will be carrying out later this morning. I want to arrive at the trailhead no later than 9 a.m., but first, J and I need to take the dogs to the kennel.

I open the campervan door and see that J is starting to get up and Striker is moving around, looking to get out of the van. I place Stormy on his doggie bed outside, tied to the picnic table and put on water for tea while J takes Striker for his walk. Sheer excitement is starting to take over my body and I'm shimmy dancing in and out of the van. I can't wait.

When J gets back, I say, "We've got to head out around 9 a.m." She looks at me and says that she doesn't think she wants to go. I keep my face expressionless and just look at her for a couple of seconds. "Why?" I finally ask.

"I just don't think they'll be okay at the kennel," she says, "and I don't want to leave them there."

I'm so disappointed, but I shake my head and say, "Not a problem—I understand." Part of me *does* understand why she's worried about the dogs, especially Striker. Who knows what their responses to the nearby horses might be? She would be thinking about them throughout the hike and worrying, and that would *not* be a good hike, not for me and not for her. Maybe she really doesn't want to hike, either. That's okay. After all, this half of the trip was really focused on what I wanted to do, and although I wanted to share all of the hiking experiences with her, clearly we are making adjustments as we go. She will stay behind with Stormy and Striker.

I'm a seasoned solo traveler; going out on my own is second nature to me. I pack my backpack with my full water bladder and lots of food for today's much longer hike: trail mix, leftover cold quesadillas from last night, oranges and a banana. I also have my hiking poles, rainwear and headlamp (just in case). Even though I'll be hiking solo, I'm still very eager to get going. I pet both dogs and say my goodbyes. J waves as I head off; I wave back.

I arrive at the trailhead of Mist Trail and eagerly plunge ahead. I haven't hiked more than a quarter-mile when I see a large black bear up in a tree. I freeze and can't believe my eyes. I've never seen a bear before, and this one is a *big* bear. Where are all of the hikers I've read about being on Mist Trail? This is supposed to be a popular trail, yet I'm here alone. *What should I do?* I think frantically.

I'm pretty sure the bear hasn't seen me yet. *Why didn't I read that leaflet on the bathroom door explaining what to do if you encounter a bear??* I don't have any bear spray on me, so I start to walk slowly backwards just as other hikers come from behind me. I hear screams: "It's a bear!! It's a bear!!" They pull out their phones and start to take pictures.

One girl who appears to know what she's doing starts to make a lot of noise. (That's what you're supposed to do, I read later.) As she's doing this, the bear is moving higher up the tree. He doesn't look aggressive or concerned about us. I get out my phone, take a step away from everyone and proceed to take my own photos. He's farther back in the trees now, and we're all in disbelief that we actually got to see a bear. Talk about a highlight of the hike! And I've barely started. Wow!

I'm actually getting cell coverage, so I text J "Bear!" and send her a pic before continuing along the trail. I can hear screams coming from behind me—the bear must have resurfaced. I briefly look back and then keep moving ahead.

The trail starts to climb—it's become vertical stone staircases that edge along the waterfalls. I'm now getting wet from the mist that envelopes the appropriately named Mist Trail. I stop, along with others, as we all pull out our rain jackets, and I put it over me and my backpack. The day was chilly at first, but as I climb, I'm warming up. The sun is out on the other side of the waterfall. It's shaded where I am, providing a gorgeous contrast. The higher I climb, the more hikers I see behind me. The staircase holds a mule train of people: young people, old people, a very pregnant woman (*How inspiring!* I think) and even babies in backpack carriers. The babies in carriers make me nervous—one slip and fall, and that baby is hurt.

After the long vertical climb, I reach the top of Vernal Fall. It's a breakpoint where hikers are sitting and lying on a granite slab. It's a grand viewpoint! There's even a rainbow along the waterfall. I'm in heaven… but I'm also quite hungry. I get out my food and sit down alongside dozens of other hikers. Everyone is taking lots of waterfall pictures. I look around, taking it all in. Nature is fabulous! I wouldn't have missed this for anything. I'm sorry J can't see it—it's worth every step.

As I start to eat, I observe a couple with their teenage girls. They've spread out a large picnic blanket and a lavish lunch spread of chicken sandwiches, quinoa salad and fruit. They ask if I'd like to join them. "Of course!" I say with a big smile. They're a wonderful family from San Diego who are avid hikers. We talk about hiking in general and what we've seen thus far at Yosemite. Hiking creates a special camaraderie, and it's very easy to spend time sharing our mutual love of hiking, nature, national parks and especially Yosemite.

After a thirty-minute lunch break with this lovely family, I begin the second part of the hike and head for Nevada Fall. It's another 600-foot vertical climb. At this stage, most hikers have headed back down, so the trail is much less crowded. It's harder going, but I'm able to capture photos of Emerald Pool and Silver Apron, both gorgeous pools of water. The trail continues with switchbacks—it's quite rocky and steep. My legs are definitely feeling it! But the views of Yosemite Valley and Half Dome are mind-blowing. I pause, staring at Half Dome, thinking, *I hope I have a chance to summit you. You're a beauty.*

I get to the end of the trail and reach the footbridge crossing the Merced River above Nevada Fall. Once again, I stop to take a nice long break. This trail is the halfway point for the long Half Dome summit tomorrow—that is, if I get my permit—and I feel really good about how I've reacted to the altitude and the elevation of the climb thus far. I'm meditating, happily not too tired, and inspired by everything I'm feeling and sensing. Once again, the scenery is even more than I expected! Its enchantment is enveloping my entire soul… nature never ceases to amaze me. My emotions are immediate, but I know the feelings will last forever.

The hike down is definitely challenging for the knees, but fortunately, my hiking poles always help. As I descend, my phone regains cell coverage, and I see that I've gotten an email from the park telling me that yes, I've got a permit to hike Half Dome tomorrow. *OMG, OMG, OMG!!!!* is all I can think. Tears of joy prick my eyes. I'll be climbing this exact trail again tomorrow… and then I'll be able to keep going all the way to the summit.

As I get near the morning's bear-sighting spot, I start to walk very briskly. I don't see any other hikers, but I don't see any bears, either—all appears to be clear. I am out of the Mist Trail! I've made it!! I'm exhausted, yet also immensely satisfied. All hikers feel this way once they've completed their big hikes. It's a sense of accomplishment and success, of relishing the journey and gaining the prize of reaching the top of the trail.

It's a euphoric feeling. In all my years of hiking, I've never tired of this very specific feeling that you can't capture by doing anything else. Some people might wonder why anyone would carry a bunch of stuff on their back, climb uphill for hours (sometimes in rain, wind, mud, ice, snow, you name it) just to summit and hit a literal high point. I do it because what the hike teaches you along the way is a metaphor for life.

After four full hours, I'm back at the campsite, my knees sore thanks to all of the downhill hiking. I see J reading on the camping chair and the two dogs lying asleep beside her. What a peaceful sight. I run up to her and jump up and down. "I got the permit for Half Dome! I got it!!" She gets up and gives me a big hug, knowing what this means for me.

She's spent her day doing yoga, meditating, walking the dogs and reading. Now she's totally relaxed and in her own state of Zen. "How was the hike?" she inquires.

I sit on the picnic bench and start to slowly untie my shoelaces off my hiking boots. "It was amazing! It was a grand day. I'm sorry you couldn't experience it, but it was wonderful. And I took lots of photos." I tell her about the bear sighting and how crazy (and scary) that was to see. After we catch up on each other's day, though, all I can think about is how much I want to take a shower.

It's been three days since my last shower. I tell her I'm going to use the campervan shower, but she says that it's not working well. "I think the drain must be clogged," she explains. "When I tried taking a shower earlier today, it started to flood the entire toilet area—I had to bucket the water out by hand into the sink."

"Oh, gross," I say, disappointed. I decide to skip the shower idea. J suggests doing a sink wash instead, but frankly, I have no desire to use the shower or the toilet area in the van unless it's absolutely necessary. I keep thinking about the black water that has to be emptied. *So Gross...* I'll just sink-wash in the park bathroom.

A little later on, I've washed as best I can and changed my clothes. I feel a little cleaner and have gotten a second wind. Cocktail hour is upon us! We open a bottle of chardonnay and chat more about our day. We had two very different days, but still, we had lots of perfectly matched moments in terms of our inner bliss: hers came when she did yoga and spent time with the dogs at the campsite, and mine came on top of Nevada Fall as I was soaking in everything Mother Earth had to offer.

Tonight, we have a few new neighbors, including a young, adorable couple named George and Angel who are traveling with their two dogs in a retrofitted van. They're very interested in the campervan, so we give them a tour of its interior. They're quite impressed. On the other side, our new neighbors are three avid hikers from Israel. They'll be heading up to Half Dome in a couple of days. They offer us juicy, delicious slices of watermelon, and we talk for a while, with me sharing how thrilled and surprised I was to receive my hiking lottery permit.

Cocktail hour has become dinner hour, and together, J and I prepare an easy vegetable stir-fry. I inhale the food. It's delicious! I may have beaten Striker's record of taking less than thirty seconds to wipe my bowl clean. The moderate to strenuous hike definitely kicked my appetite into high gear.

As the park gets dark, Angel grabs a couple of hula hoops, including one that has LED lighting, that she keeps in the back of their van and starts to move the hoops around her hips and arms and neck. She's quite good! No, she's really good. And, who knew hula hoops now have lighting?! She asks if we want to try. I'm too tired. J stands up and starts working her hips. After a few tries, she's getting the hang of it, keeping the hoop up and near her mid-section. George is acting DJ and plays music for us—a combination of Nineties and Noughties alternative rock—as Angel and J provide us with a hula entertainment show. Other campers nearby are also enjoying the scene.

George and I stretch out in our camping chairs as Angel and J keep hula-hooping. He tells me about their fascinating road trip visiting numerous national parks, that started three months ago in Baltimore and will end in Vancouver. I sip wine and he drinks beer as we share our passions for road trips and hikes. What a nice couple, so glad we met them—the joys of travel!

By the end of the night, J proclaims that she will be buying some hula hoops soon. Meanwhile tonight, the dogs have remained rather sedate; I think they're still recovering from yesterday's hike. It's been a long day, and tomorrow will be even longer—it's a twelve-hour hike to Half Dome, so I've got to get started before sunrise in order to get back before it's dark. I call it an early evening and wish everyone goodnight. I get into the tent, set my alarm, lay down on my mat, slip into my sleeping bag and quickly fall asleep. I can't wait for tomorrow.

Chapter 12

Half Dome

HEN MY PHONE alarm goes off at 5 a.m., I'm immediately awake. Half Dome is the main reason I wanted to come to Yosemite! It's been on my bucket list for over a decade, and thanks to sheer luck, today is the day. Finally, I have an opportunity to climb this iconic landmark! It sits 4,800 feet above where we are now in Yosemite Valley and 8,800 feet above sea level. The challenge is not only the distance of the seventeen-mile round trip, it's also the elevation of those granite slabs—the climb creates some very slippery sections, especially at the top where two metal cables and wooden planks have been placed for the last 400 feet. And then there are the winds (and occasionally lightning) that can create dangerous conditions. Hikers have died on the trail, mainly during spells of wet weather. I'm very mindful of the conditions and will definitely respect how Mother Nature may alter my plans.

I didn't sleep much because I was so pumped up about the hike. I've read about hikers using the cables that are attached to the rock during the last parts of the ascent, and I keep visualizing what it might be like to keep my footing on the granite floor while pulling myself along the cables. I jump out of my sleeping bag and start getting dressed. Again, I layer my clothes. It's very cold right now, probably the coldest it's been the entire trip—it's only in the high thirties. Better dress in five layers to start! I can peel them off once I start to warm up as I climb.

It's still very dark out, and it's eerily quiet, too. I head to the bathroom to wash up and ironically see the bear leaflet again on the wall. This time, I stop to read it in great detail. I doubt I'll experience a second bear sighting, but then again, who knows? My next step is to fill up my water bladder completely. I'll be carrying about a gallon of water, which is a lot, but then again, I'll be hiking all day. The key will be staying hydrated.

I return to my tent and fill my backpack with lots of food and snacks, including energy bars, oranges, trail mix and a couple of hard-boiled eggs I made last night. I find the gloves that I purchased specifically for the cables and add them to the backpack. Given how dark it is, I strap on my headlamp, too. *Okay… I think I have everything.*

It's now 6 a.m. and time to get started—I don't want to leave too late given the fact that it could storm in the afternoon and how dark it could get as I'm hiking back. I open the campervan door and let J know I'm leaving.

"Good luck!" she says, and gets out of bed to stumble over to the door and give me a big hug. She knows how important this venture is to me. Stormy's awake, too, and has jumped off of the sofa to come over to the door. I give him a big hug, knowing that he thinks it's time for our morning walk. "Not this morning, Stormy," I tell him with a smile. "J will walk you today."

I slide the door shut and head out of our campsite, but I've only gotten a few steps before I stop, thinking about Stormy and the fact that he's accustomed to our morning walk at this hour. I'm feeling guilty. *I can't just leave him!* I keep thinking. I rush back to the van and open the door again. "Let me take him out for a quick walk," I say.

J looks surprised. "Are you sure? I can walk him."

I shake my head. "No, he's grown used to our walk." I grab his leash, pull the step down for him and take him around the campgrounds. His practice of smelling every bush, every tree, every plant continues…it's mind-blowing how quickly dogs create a happy routine. At his ripe age, Stormy continues to take relish in this new, natural world that puts him in a state of utter joy. But I've got to head out! I didn't want to leave this late—it could be a major problem on the way back. I rush him back to the van, open the door and push him in. "Okay, now I'm off!" I get another hug and round of well-wishes from J.

My adventure now begins. I head back to yesterday's trailhead, beginning at Happy Isle and continuing on to Mist Trail. I could come back a different way by taking the John Muir Trail down from Vernal Fall, but it's quite a bit longer, so I'll have to scrap that view on this trip. As I did yesterday, I'll be visiting Vernal Fall and Nevada Fall on my way to Half Dome.

I haven't seen any other hikers on the trail yet, and I gingerly walk past where I saw the bear yesterday, relieved when I don't see any traces of him (her?). I finally do see a handful of other hikers as I cross the Vernal Fall footbridge. They're climbing the stairs to the right of the waterfall. The scattered hikers make for quite a different scene than the long trail I saw of people yesterday! The ones here today are mainly headed to Half Dome, and they look serious, fit, determined and full of energy. We all have a shared mission: to summit Half Dome, safely return and proudly proclaim it for all the world to hear!!!

The steep granite stairway begins, and so does the enveloping mist from the waterfall. Once again at this stage, I get out my rainwear and put it over myself and my backpack. No StairMaster could do to your legs what this is doing right now! But I take it nice and slow as it's very slippery. *How do people wearing only gym shoes or running shoes make it up this trail?* I wonder as I see some people wearing exactly that. I don't know.

I arrive at the top of Vernal Fall again, but this time, I only pause for a few minutes, just long enough to drink some water and eat an energy bar. This is so unlike yesterday, when I leisurely took in the sights and enjoyed the journey to the top of the falls. Today, I'm hustling past the two viewpoints I visited yesterday so that I can start the ascent to the top of Half Dome.

Although the sun is out, I start to see dark clouds forming over the valley. Rather than let myself worry, though, I center my mind on the trail and continue on to Nevada Fall, again passing Emerald Pool and Silver Apron. I reach the top of the footbridge and see that the dark clouds are now in full swing over me. Okay, now I'm concerned. This is the one thing that has worried me the most about the hike: the afternoon weather patterns bringing in rain and perhaps lightning. I need to stop and eat to keep my energy level high, but I'm now beginning to worry about those clouds. I grab the eggs and trail mix and devour the food as fast as I can, downing it with gulps of water. Timing is now a factor, I know, but I also know that I can't sprint my way to the top—this is a hike, not a race.

A couple approaches me at the footbridge. They're also headed to Half Dome and are wondering about the same thing I'm wondering about: can we hike to Half Dome and back prior to what appears to be rainfall approaching? They blurt out what no one really wants to say, which is, "Should we turn back?" When I hear those words spoken aloud, I feel tears forming in my eyes and my chest starting to pulsate with fear. *Not summiting?? How can we not summit when we're so close?*

We all look at each other, knowing that we're feeling exactly the same way. I shake my head no. "We should continue," I say. "I don't want to turn back." We keep staring at the darkening clouds. We are only halfway to the summit—we still have a long way to go. The decision has to be made quickly.

After about five more minutes of thought, I decide to carry on, and they decide to head back down. It's a very difficult decision for each of us. There's still a lot of trail to hike, and I'm hoping there might be some improvement in the weather by the time I reach the cables. *Sometimes you have to keep moving forward, I think. Besides, there's little risk at this point—the major decision will come at the start of the cables, because if it is raining at all, slippery conditions will make summiting very problematic if not impossible.*

I push onward, but I feel a heaviness in my head, heart and step. I am definitely worried. Not scared, but worried. I keep going, though, hiking to Liberty Cap and through the sequoia forest. It's a gorgeous, steady uphill walk, and I can see Half Dome peeking through the trees. Unfortunately, the dark clouds are not going away. My pending decision is weighing on me. *Do I turn back here or keep moving towards Sub Dome? That's supposed to be the hardest part of the hike.* I decide I'll make the final call at the start of Sub Dome.

I reach the base of Sub Dome and see that the clouds are turning even darker. The few hikers around me decide to turn back. It's too dangerous to continue—from all indications, it's about to rain, maybe even storm. It just wasn't meant to be. I glance up at Sub Dome with tears flowing down my cheeks. All of the planning, the anticipation, the mental and physical struggle just to get to this point…and I've got to turn back. I know it's the right decision, but it's so damn disheartening.

Three more hikers approach me. They were at the cables, they tell me, but they turned around. "It's too dangerous to continue," they warn me. It's just not the day for Half Dome.

I continue to look up, part of me still in disbelief. I usually enjoy solo travel, but not now. This is a time when being alone truly sucks. An utter sadness overcomes me; I can't tear my eyes away from Half Dome. After a couple of minutes, though, I start to head back down the trail, dejected. My eyes are swollen as I slog through Nevada Fall and then Vernal Fall.

A slight mist begins to drop down from the dark clouds. I definitely made the right call. Now the staircase leading down past Vernal Fall is very slippery and wet, making it a torturously slow hike back. I finally reach the trailhead of Mist Trail. I stop and look back again. I tried… it just wasn't meant to be, not today, not on this trip. As a hiker, it's very important to know when to turn back. Half Dome will continue to be on my bucket list.

Time to get back to the campsite—I need a drink, and I'm starved. I see the familiar red campervan with J, Striker and Stormy outside of it. I'm so happy to see them! We've become a family during the past few days, and I really could use their support right now. J says that our campsite neighbors had heard that hikers were returning off from Half Dome without summiting. "I was worried about you!" she says.

I tell her all about the journey and that I wasn't meant to summit Half Dome today. She opens a bottle of wine, pours a glass and says, "You're amazing for trying that climb—who does that solo and at our age?"

I tear up again and declare, "Well, I wasn't the oldest hiker on the trail. I'm not a dinosaur!" We laugh.

Before we make dinner, we take Stormy and Striker for their late afternoon walk. My legs are sore. J and

I continue to talk about the day's journey and she attempts to console me, but what helps the most is that she is here and the dogs are here and I'm not feeling alone.

We return back to our campsite. J heads to the bear locker and pulls out the dog food and I start making dinner. After the dogs are fed, J starts the campfire. The way we address our tasks and seamlessly take on what needs to be done has almost become a rhythmic dance. Through non-verbal means, we have created a harmonious process and flow. It's quite fascinating, really. The true definition of teamwork.

It's our last night at Yosemite. Our previous camping neighbors George and Angel left earlier today. People come and people go…it's part of traveling. When it comes to some people, though, memories do remain. The three Israeli hikers are still here, and they're looking forward to their attempt at Half Dome tomorrow. I wish them well and hope they have a successful summit. If the weather cooperates, they'll be fine.

J and I are celebrating in spite of my Half Dome bitter disappointment. We've experienced an awe-inspiring nature's wonderland, the dogs have uncovered a renewed sense of energy we didn't think they had and the comfort our campervan has given us has proven to be well worth the added expense.

And besides, we've just started this road trip. We're both looking forward to more.

Chapter 13

Shower

MORNING SOUNDS WAKE me up at 6 a.m., and as I look around my tent, I can see traces of day-light. This is the longest I've slept during the last four nights at Yosemite! I hear the sounds of voices, cars starting and muffled movements, but I just lie there. I'm in no hurry to get up and out this morning—the only thing on my agenda is Stormy's walk. For a brief moment, my thoughts center themselves on yesterday and my missed attempt at summiting Half Dome, but I quickly divert my thoughts—no sense in reliving that sadness. After ten minutes of just lying in the tent and listening to the sounds outside of it, I finally jump out of my sleeping bag, put on a semi-fresh pair of pants and pullover, unzip the tent and squeeze out.

I head to the van and slide open the door. On this last morning at Yosemite, J, Striker and Stormy are all up and ready to get out. "Good morning!" I say to everyone, then to Stormy I say, "Shall we all go for our morning walk, together?" J and I leash the dogs, and then we all pile out of the van.

It's another crisp, chilly morning, but the dogs are in a great mood and walking along swiftly. Do they know this is their last day here? Striker is bouncing along with his three-and-a-half legs, the cone hopping up and down his neck in tandem with his hippity-hop pace. Stormy, too, is moving with alacrity compared to when we all hiked together a few days ago. They're happy, high-spirited and roaming with a sense of purpose.

We head to Half Dome Village, where I stop at the coffee shop and pick up our drinks. There's a veranda nearby with rocking chairs, so J and I take a seat and hope the dogs will do the same. The sun is shining brightly. What a perfect sunny morning! But despite the gorgeous setting, a slight melancholic feeling settles upon me. I can barely believe we're leaving today. I look around and think, *I'm going to miss this place.*

On our way back, we cross over to Cook's Meadow Loop and follow the wooden path back to the campsite. It's a flat, easy hike that takes us through a pair of meadows. Once again, there's Half Dome. As we walk, we encounter deer and their fawns, prompting Striker to start jumping wildly towards them. Thank goodness, Stormy is less animated given his age, but he wants to go there, too. We hold on tightly to their leashes.

After our two-mile walk back to the van, we start to break down our campsite. First, J feeds the dogs their last Yosemite meal as I begin to break down my tent, which is an easy ten-minute task. I'm not hungry this morning, so I'll be skipping breakfast. J grabs yogurt and fruit from the fridge while the dogs are having their breakfast. After the dogs are fed, we roll up the awning, fold up the camping chairs and rug, and stow away the dog accessories, tent, sleeping bag and hiking poles in the rear storage carrier. Checkout is 11 a.m., and it's getting to be that time. We start to drive out of Yosemite Valley.

I could stay here another week. I could come here every few months and experience Yosemite in every season. *Next time, I'll come for seven days*, I vow. *Hopefully I'll get another crack at Half Dome if I'm lucky enough to secure another permit.* There's so much yet to see and there are so many trails to hike! I fell totally in love with this place. But J is ready to go—four days was plenty for her.

I'm driving again; at this point, I'm unquestionably the designated driver. Before we head out of the park, we stop by the tank station to empty the gray and black water tanks and refill them with fresh (though undrinkable) water. This is our first time dealing with the tanks, so I'm just hoping for the best. J gets the pair of latex gloves out of the small box on the side of the van and pulls out the hose. She connects it and opens up the ground hole cover, then turns the van's knob. It's working—yay! We can tell it's working, because the smell is vile. I'm so glad that I've got driving duty and she's taken on this odorous task. Once the emptying is done, I refill the water tanks on the other side, a less smelly and easier task. Wow! We did it!

As we leave the park, we wave and chorus, "Good-bye, Yosemite!" What a grand time! Once out of Yosemite, we start heading north on Route 120 West towards Jackson, where J has plans to meet friends for lunch prior to the big reunion party that'll be happening later tonight. According to the Waze app, we've got a two-hour drive. The dogs are in their designated places: Stormy's on the sofa and Striker's on the bed in the back. Everyone seems comfortable, so we put on my playlist and continue our road trip. My alternative music channel includes Foals, Cage the Elephant, Arctic Monkeys, Arcade Fire and Milky Chance. I'm feeling really good and J is starting to get excited about the lunch, the reunion party and seeing her old friends.

Now we're descending 1,000 feet, crossing a scenic lake near Oakdale. I've never heard of Lake Don Pedro. It's small but pristine. This is a little gem of California that I didn't know about! We keep driving, passing through fruit orchards and dairy towns. Waze has navigated us onto a country road where we don't see any other vehicles—we're the only ones.

I look at J and ask, "How did we get here?"

She checks her phone and shrugs. "This is where Waze said to go."

I frown. "But how can this be the right way?" We're in the middle of dairy country; all we can see are cows and barns. It's really pretty and scenic, but are we lost? We decide to stop and double-check the app. Rather than pull over, we just stop in the middle of the two-lane road because there's no one else around to worry about.

While we've stopped, we also take some pictures. Lots of pictures, actually. We let the dogs out and they try to rush towards the cows, but we pull back on their leashes. They complete their business and we circle with them around the van. This is definitely off the beaten path, but we like it. For a moment, we just keep looking around us in circles. Sometimes it's good to get lost.

Then a pickup truck finally does come along. It stops in front of us, and the driver gets out to ask if we're okay. We say yes, thank you, we're fine, but we do seem to be lost. He gives us some directions and we all get back into the van. There's no cell service here, so we follow his directions and get to San Andreas, California. The only thing I know about San Andreas is that it's the major earthquake fault line. "So, *this* is where it is," I tell J as we drive through. There doesn't seem to be anything special about it—we don't see any markers or road signs talking about the San Andreas

Fault. I'm just hoping there isn't an earthquake while we're at the potential epicenter.

Due to our little misdirection, J's going to be late for her lunch. She texts her friends and gives them a new time, then goes to the back of the van and starts putting on make-up and changing her clothes. She looks good! You'd never know she's just come back from a four-day Yosemite trip. She hasn't seen these friends in over twenty years—it's a pre-reunion of sorts before tonight's big reunion party. While she's having lunch, I'm going to keep an eye on the dogs and maybe try to rinse off some of my accumulated Yosemite dirt in the van's tiny bathroom sink.

We finally get to Jackson, where they're waiting for her in a hotel bar. I find a large Dollar Store parking lot across the street. I park at the edge of the lot where there are no other vehicles, and she rushes out. I take a moment to stretch and relax, knowing I've got a couple of hours to wait. I badly want to rinse off some of my dirt. But, first things first: the dogs. I put on their leashes and we walk around the lot where there are some pathetic-looking bushes and plants. I'm sure the dogs are wondering how we've ended up here. *What happened to all of those amazing smells from Yosemite?* is probably what they're thinking. Nonetheless, they obligingly do their business, and I rush them back into the van.

Now it's time for me to clean up as best I can. I put both dogs on the sofa, placing them as far apart as possible. I'm praying they can behave themselves. "No fighting!" I say aloud to them.

I head back to the bathroom area and take off my clothes. When I attempt to pull the door shut, I find out it's stuck. *Guess I'll have an audience…* But that doesn't turn out to be my main problem, because when I turn on the water, the hand-held showerhead wildly sprays water all over. "No, no, no!" I gasp out loud. Water is everywhere: on the bed, all over the floor, trickling down the bathroom walls. This attempt at a shower is a disaster! The dogs are staring intensely, thinking *what is she doing*. They're so focused on me, they've avoided fighting over the sofa territory.

Time to improvise and do what J had suggested earlier. I turn on the sink and scrub a bar of soap quickly over my body, then use a washcloth to rinse off. I don't have time to wash my hair, so it'll have to stay dirty. At least I can toss it into a top bun. I feel somewhat better, but not much. It's just going to have to do for now.

Trying to do all of this with the dogs staring at me is making me uncomfortable. I'm a bit shy. I'm also trying to hurry because I'm concerned that J may bring her friends back to the van to check it out, in which case they'll find me butt-naked and wet. Plus, seeing the two dogs together on the sofa will make her worry that they might get into another scuffle. She likes to keep them separated. I check the time and go from hurrying to madly rushing.

Finally, I'm finished! I towel off and throw on some semi-fresh clothes. I'm pretty sure I've only worn this shirt and these pants twice—they only have a somewhat stinky smell. Just as I start to towel-dry the water that sprayed across the entire bathroom and bedroom area, J slides open the van door and I hear lots of voices. "Come on in, here it is..."

The dogs jump up and rush towards her in a mad dash. I just put my hand on my hip, toss my head back and say, "Hello!" Two people have come into the front of the van and two more are outside peering in to see the set-up. Because of Striker's dog crate, I can't exit the back, where I am now stuck.

I smile and let them know I just rinsed off. "It's a bit wet back here," I warn them. Besides that, the back is stuffed with our luggage, backpacks and dog crate, plus there are towels and clothes hanging everywhere. In short, it's a god-awful mess... but still, they're really impressed. (And I'm relieved that they didn't walk into a more embarrassing scene.) After some conversation about how much we and the dogs enjoyed Yosemite, they say they'll see us again later. The scene is so chaotic that I don't get anyone's name.

I ask J where the reunion party is. "It's at my friend Josh's house, and we'll be able to park the campervan there. You can put your tent up, too," she reports happily. She really wants me to attend the party with her, but I politely decline and say that I've already got plans.

"You've got all your friends and classmates there—it'll be fun!" I say.

"What are you going to do?" she inquires.

I wink. "I may have a date," I say.

Chapter 14

Online Dating

FOR THE PAST six months, I've been on an online dating site that's marketed specifically to women. It all started when I was at my health club and overheard two younger women talking about their dates and how they each met the guys online. "It's a numbers game," one said to the other. I'd heard about this app a year ago and was intrigued because it allows the woman to control the initial contact. Hearing about their successes finally encouraged me to download the app and set up my own profile.

It's time to get back onto the dating scene, I said to myself. It had been four years since my last relationship, and that one hadn't ended very well. Dating is work! Lots of work. Where do you find a pool of potential candidates? Not in bars—that has all dried up. In our new world, online dating is where to go. But how do you find a normal person who isn't fake, who enjoys the majority of the same things you enjoy, is rather good-looking and is within your age range? That's a rhetorical question, of course—there are lots of people who have been successful with online dating. It would be nice to share a cocktail on a weekend night with someone whom I find interesting and who finds me interesting.

So, I decided, *what do I have to lose, I'll try.* Once I had set up my profile, I immediately saw profiles of twenty guys accompanied by their small bio pictures. Apparently, they had expressed an interest in contacting me. Woo-hoo! I was totally new to the swipe-left-swipe-right concept—probably accidentally reversed it the first few tries. I was impressed with seeing twenty men right away… until I read their bio descriptions and couldn't believe some of the things I was reading. "I'm married. My wife knows I'm here, and I just want a sexual relationship with someone else," some of the profiles read. Some men even had their wife with them in their photos. One man laid out in great detail what he expected: everything from the woman's physical appearance and how he would want her to shave to where he was willing to travel and how many times per week he was available. It didn't take me long to realize that there are three kinds of guys on dating apps: men who only want sex (from quick booty calls to full-on affairs), men who want long-term relationships right out of the gate, and men who are looking for companionship and are willing to be open and see where things go. I was clearly looking for the latter kind of guy.

After a month, I honestly wanted to give up, but then a few worthwhile guys began to appear, so I gave them a try. *Some have promise*, I thought. I started to chat via the app, then moved to texting, then finally to phone conversations. I went out for a couple of coffees and dinners, but nothing moved forward past the first or second date.

Then a guy who was very cute but who lived in the San Francisco area appeared. Apparently, he was within my mile range at one point while I was on a business trip, and we somehow connected through a series of app chats and then text messages. His name was Antonio. He was a cyclist with lovely blue eyes who loved the outdoors and was a few years younger than me, and he was divorced with two grown kids. All sounds good, right? We started to upgrade to phone conversations, and by sheer circumstance, I wound up in the SF area. (That had been a few months back.) We decided to meet up for the first time over happy hour cocktails prior to my late-night return flight to Orange County. It went really well! We spent two hours together and had good chemistry and nice conversation. We both agreed that we wanted to continue talking and hopefully meet up again in southern California or again in San Francisco if I should get back to that area. I even invited him to come down to Orange County and visit me in Laguna Beach. I thought, *He's not in the area, no, but who knows what can happen?* I've had long-distance relationships in the past, so it wasn't an automatic disqualifier.

As luck would have it, this road trip was going to include the Bay Area, so I sent him a text telling him exactly when I would be available to meet up, namely the evening of J's reunion party. He was very excited and said to text me the day of my arrival so that we could coordinate where to meet for dinner. I was really looking forward to seeing him again. I'd even packed a nice BLD (black little dress) for the date and had kept it buried at the very bottom of my backpack.

Fast-forward to today. I text him while I'm in the Dollar Store parking lot, telling him how great Yosemite was and reminding him that I'll be nearby this evening and can meet him for dinner. "Could you suggest a good meeting place?" I text. "I plan on taking an Uber."

Given all that's happened since I had texted him earlier in the day, I haven't had a chance to check for a reply, but I'm sure he has responded—it's now been a couple of hours. I look at my phone… and see nothing. No response yet. *Hmm… I'm sure he's busy,* I think. By the time we arrive at Josh's house for the reunion party, Antonio should have responded with a meeting place.

We leave Jackson on Route 88 and drive through Lodi on Route 12. It's wine country interspersed with some robust cherry orchards. It's a real treat to take an undiscovered path! We end up at the house in Brentwood, with a view of Mount Diablo, and are directed to park the campervan at the front of the property. Apparently, I'll be setting up my tent practically at the outskirts of the fire pit ring that's surrounded by a circle of cushioned swings. Music, food and drinks are being set up nearby.

J is anxious to catch up with her former classmates and do what one typically does at reunions: rehash the high-school years and talk about their lives in between. She eagerly begins to greet people who approach the campervan as they enter the property. The van has become one of the meet-and-greet sites! For the first time, we're able to plug the campervan into an electrical outlet versus using the noisy generator, allowing for the interior lights to be on throughout the night. We are a beacon of greeting.

It's 6 p.m., and I've given up on having a date with Antonio. *What a jerk!* I think to myself. Finally, he texts: "Sorry, can't meet, my sister is in town."

What?? I reread the message. *Well, this is pathetic—it's the sister excuse.* I know she lives in another country. *And the jerk didn't even have the guts to call? Instead, he just texts?* I read his message again and again, trying to square our first meeting and all of the communication we had in between with today's text rejection. *How did I misread him?* I can only shake my head. I'd like to crawl into a hole right now, but I'm surrounded by people; I want to slip into my tent, but how strange would that look at 6 p.m.?

I'm in no mood for being at a party or meeting new people, but I don't want to be rude, either. The tent is practically between the front of the house and the fire pit, and this spot seems to be where everyone appears to be congregating because of the live music.

As I'm getting the rejection text, J is completely encircled by her friends and what appear to be quite a few former and current admirers. She is by far the most youthful and pretty woman here—no one else comes close. The guys are all clamoring to spend time with her. She's the belle of the ball having a grand ol' time! Meanwhile, I've had my first online dating app rejection. A tale of two women.

I grab the dogs, put on their leashes and head to the dirt road to take them for a long walk. The road goes for about a quarter-mile. I wish it went on for a mile or two miles or more. I could walk forever right now. It's bordered by a fence on the left; I see horses roaming and grazing. The dogs are trying to stay on the right—I think they're a little frightened by the horses. It's a nice, pleasant walk, except for the dirt that's blowing as cars pass on their way to Josh's house.

Thank goodness for the dogs! I needed an excuse to get away from the party so that I can process everything that's happened with Antonio. I'm feeling slightly hurt and quite bewildered, rejected and disappointed… but deep down, I'm not surprised. The online dating thing has always made me hesitate. Frankly, whenever I've started to talk to someone, I've always felt like I was just waiting for a shoe to drop. It just did. Something strange is going on with this Antonio situation, but right now, I only want to get through the evening, maybe have a drink when I get back to the van, and hopefully be able to sleep. Given the party scene, that may not be so easy—I sense there are some serious partygoers here. It's going to be a long night.

J sees me walking back with the dogs and asks, "Are you staying? Please stay!"

"Yes," I say, "I'm staying." To my relief, she doesn't inquire too much more about the potential date. I try to put the dogs back into the van, but they're too energized for that, so we head to the swings next to the fire pit instead. The live music is really good! That's a pleasant surprise.

Stormy is behaving well—he's just lying on the cushioned swing with me and observing the partygoers. Striker, of course, is jumping up and down, and his cone keeps banging against swings, poles and people trying to get by. J is enmeshed in deep conversations. Someone brings me a glass of red wine, and I want to kiss him. "Thank you!" I say.

Eventually, even Striker begins to settle down. Both dogs and I enjoy the singer. He has a great voice and is covering songs by U2, Tom Petty, Neil Young and Johnny Cash. I'm so happy for the distraction. *What would I do without this music tonight?* I wonder.

J comes by and sits down with us. The warmth of the fire pit is making our faces glow, and we're both a little buzzed. "How's it going?" she asks.

I shout, "Antonio proved to be an ass, but I'm happy to be here!" We clink our wine glasses and both say "Cheers!" I have a big smile on my face now.

With J right next to them, both dogs are staying completely calm. That doesn't last long, however—pretty soon, she's pulled to her feet by an old friend who wants to show her his new motorcycle. Striker clearly wants to go with her, but I tell her, "I've got the dogs—go ahead."

It's now almost 10 p.m., and with the few glasses of red wine I've had, I'm ready for bed. I let J know that I'm heading for my tent. On the way, I put both dogs into the campervan, Striker in the crate and Stormy on the sofa bed. I slide the van door shut and hope that the noise still coming from the party won't be too loud for them.

I unzip the tent fly and dive in. I can still hear the party noise, yes, but that's all right. My backpack is already inside the tent. I turn on my headlamp, reach inside and pull out my pajama T-shirt and shorts. Quickly, I change into them and jump into my sleeping bag, where I look at my phone and read that text message again. *Unbelievable…*

I close my eyes and fall asleep.

Chapter 15

Silicon Valley

WHEN I WAKE up the next morning, the sunlight is piercing the tent. And, it's warm. I slept outside my sleeping bag last night, it was just too warm. What a difference from Yosemite's campsite! I look at my phone and see another text message from Antonio. He's apologized for not being able to see me, but he says his "fiancée" would not have understood. WHAT!?! What fiancée? Since when was there a *fiancée*? He sent this message at midnight, presumably when she was asleep and he had the opportunity to text. I'm beyond outraged. This is online dating?? I'm done!

I text back, "Delete any and all messages from me and delete my phone number. I'm blocking you! You're pathetic."

It's 7 a.m. already. Time to walk Stormy and Striker! No doubt J is sleeping in late.

I unzip the tent, stick my head out and look around to see nothing but empty bottles of beer, wine and liquor circling the yard. The large garbage bins are overflowing with rubbish and bottles. When I open the van door, Stormy's wide awake and ready to head out. He's apparently been waiting quite patiently. Striker is moving around in the back in his crate, too. I hold Stormy in the van with one hand as I climb inside and open Striker's crate. Both are anxious to get out—it's late for their morning walk. I see the back of J's head planked into her pillow. She's out!

I leash both dogs, quietly shut the door after they're out and start their walks. I'm in my pajama shorts with flip-flops on my feet and sunglasses on my face. The dogs are scrambling around, making their leashes cross as they start to do their business on whatever bushes they can smell. We walk the full quarter-mile to the road. Once again, they see the horses on the left and remain on the right side. Still scared, I guess.

It's a pleasant, balmy, sunny California morning, although I'm starting to hear fertilizer planes flying overhead. When I get back to the van, J has gotten up, started her coffeemaker and is pulling out the large bag of dog food. As soon as they see her and smell their food, they sit anxiously right next to her, waiting for their bowls to be filled.

"Good morning!" I say. "How did you sleep?" She definitely had a long night: her eyes are tired, her face is crumpled, her clothes are wrinkled.

"I drank too much," she says, unsurprisingly.

I smile. "That's okay! What else are you going to do when you attend a reunion party?"

As she feeds the dogs, I get into the van and heat water to make chamomile tea. Along with the tea, I throw some granola in a bowl and pour on a splash of almond milk. We're both outside in the front yard when her friends come out of the house with large black garbage bags and start to pick up the bottles.

I head back to the tent, change into whatever clothes smell best and then begin to tear down the tent while J and her friends chat about last night. It's the post-reunion party review interspersed with bits of gossip.

J and I both would like to take a proper shower in the house before our next stop in Silicon Valley, but the line of leftover partygoers waiting to get into the bathroom is just too long. Plus, I'd like to get an early start—it's approximately a two-hour ride.

We thank her friends very much for their hospitality and restart our road trip. We're off to Atherton in Silicon Valley to have a scheduled lunch with Alex, our co-founder. On the way there, we text him and ask if we can stop by his house in advance to take a quick shower. He texts us back "No problem." Excellent!

As we drive along, J starts to tell me about her evening after I had gone to bed. She had a really good time and is so glad she came. "Thank you for staying last night!" she says. She pauses, then asks, "What happened to the date?"

I can feel my eyes narrowing. "I got another text late last night about a 'fiancée,'" I answer. "What's wrong with people? I don't get it! I had no idea… was it a game? I don't know and honestly, I really am over it now."

We exchange a quiet glance, shaking our heads. "Wow," she finally says.

"I'm done with online dating," I say with disgust. "I've uninstalled the app."

———————

If Silicon Valley had a Beverly Hills, this would be it: the neighborhood consists of rich, stately homes behind either gates or high hedges that protect the homeowners' privacy. This is the home of the who's who of Silicon Valley. When Alex recently built his new home, he equipped it with all of the technological gadgets you could imagine being in a "smart" home. The purpose of our visit is to not only catch up on any news (really, there isn't any) but more importantly to say hello while we're in the neighborhood. He said he'd go to the office early that day and return early to meet us at his house. After that, we're planning a quick lunch in nearby San Mateo.

We turn into his driveway off a main road. The house is gigantic and beautiful; we had expected nothing less. We get out with the dogs and let them do their business in his front yard. When we ring the bell, Alex promptly answers the door. He looks at us, his eyes quickly moving up and down, and I can tell what he's thinking—we are no doubt a mess. My hair is swept up in a top bun, I haven't washed this morning, and I'm wearing really wrinkled clothes that have been crushed inside of a backpack for five days. J looks like she's nursing a hangover—her eyes are dark with runny mascara and leftover make-up, and I don't think she's brushed her hair yet today. Striker is jumpy and seems to be saying "Who are you? Who are you?" to Alex. Stormy is totally indifferent, just sitting quietly beside me.

Yup, we're the fab four. *These are the two co-founders I've invested in??* he's probably thinking, but he says, "Hello! How are you?" He's a youthful-looking, nerdy kind of guy who wears oversized wire-rimmed glasses and only one style of pants: khakis. His wife and their little dog are gone for the weekend, he tells us, and his daughter and son are both in college out east. He's got the big house to himself.

He looks behind us and sees the red campervan. "Wow!" he says, and steps outside with wide eyes.

"That's really nice! You've been traveling in this?" He peers in and sees it all… and it's not exactly tidy in there what with the towels hanging in the back and some of J's clothes thrown on the bed.

We briefly tell him where we've been in Yosemite, the highlights of our time there, my failed attempt at Half Dome, etc. He's really intrigued by all of this. We ask if we can take a shower, and he says, "Of course, of course." J and I decide to take turns—while one of us showers, the other will stay outside and watch the dogs with Alex.

I go first, Alex leading me to a guest room and guest bathroom. No five-star hotel could be any nicer! The guest shower has more showerheads than I can count, and the temperature, texture and pressure of this water is nothing like I've ever experienced. I would forgo a month's worth of showers to experience this shower one more time—it's just that brilliant. I wash my hair and find a blow-dryer underneath a cabinet and give it a quick dry, then toss my hair back in a bun.

Meanwhile, I'm sure J is giving Alex an in-depth tour of the van's operations, no doubt including the black and gray water tank disposal process. Alex is an engineer and incredibly inquisitive, so all of the me-chanics would be quite fascinating to him. Doubtless he's asking a lot of questions.

I return to the campervan and say, "You're next!" J heads to the same guest bedroom and bathroom while

Alex and I converse about the customized construction he did on his new house and all the work and time it took to complete. It truly is a masterpiece of technology and architecture, and he's very proud of it, as he should be.

The dogs are tied to a side pole, I see. I walk over to them and untie their leashes. "Would you like to join me on a quick walk around the block while we wait for J?" I ask Alex. He nods and says yes.

We head out past the property and onto the major road. Alex's got Stormy and I've got Striker. We make small talk as we walk by more spectacular homes. It's a nice fifteen-minute walk, and we return just in time to see J coming out of the house.

My belly reminds me that we haven't eaten yet today. I'm famished, and J probably is, too. I also need my almond milk latte. We ask Alex if there's a place we can go with the dogs. He thinks a bit and says there are a few cafés with patios. It's northern California, after all. We tell him we can drive if he doesn't mind since we've got the dogs.

He gets in on the passenger side, and J goes to the sofa to sit with Stormy. Striker is alone on the bed in the back. For the first time, I realize that the camper-van smells a bit like a dog kennel. I look over at Alex and wonder if he's smelling what I'm smelling, and then I look back at J and the dogs and see that she's trying to keep them both still during the ride. At this point, I'm trying hard not to laugh.

We arrive at the café. Everybody gets out, including the dogs. We confirm that yes, it's okay to have dogs on the patio, so we sit down at a large round table. Stormy lies down near me, but Striker's trying to jump up on J's lap. The cone around his head keeps hitting the tabletop. I wonder what Alex is thinking about us fab four. We all order salads, and I order my coffee. J also asks for water for the dogs, and the waiter says, "No problem."

Alex is smiling at all of us. "I really hope the other investors come through," he says. I guess we're getting down to business.

"Well," I say, "all indications are they're very interested, but nothing can happen until they sell their other businesses. You sensed their sincerity when you spoke to them, correct? It's just going to take time."

"I know," he says. "Do you girls think there's anything more you can do in the meantime…?"

"Like what?" J asks.

I know that tone—she doesn't like the question. It's been asked over and over, and we've methodically reviewed everything that did and didn't work, spoken to hundreds of investors and decided weeks ago to wait to hear back from the one group of investors who like our new plan.

"I don't know… What do you think, girls?" Alex says. It's as if he's forgotten about all our previous conversations.

J and I exchange side looks. I say, "We've spoken to angels and VC and private equity guys, we've sent cold and warm emails to hundreds of potential investors, and we've had meetings and coffees with many of them. I mean, you know what we have: a company with a technology platform, a marketing test and not much else. There's been one investor group—and only one—who gets it. They're the only investors who are willing to put in the dollars we need to take our company down a new path." He knows all of this, of course, so I'm not sure what he's trying to say except possibly to insinuate that we haven't done enough.

The waiter brings us the water for the dogs. I reach down and give Stormy his water; J does the same for Striker. After he drinks, Stormy's mouth is filled with slimy slobber—it's a mess. He moves towards Alex, getting stringy slobber all over the bottom edges of Alex's pants. Oops! I take a napkin and very softly wipe away the slobber. I'm not sure Alex even notices.

J is sitting forward on her chair. That's not good. She says sternly, "Alex, we were counting on you to handle the financing side or to identify someone who would be interested. Luckily for us, we've been able to secure an investment interest. If the investors come through, that will be a great accomplishment." She's annoyed, and so am I.

He nods. "I understand, but this is a long shot. I'll grant that we don't have too many choices here. That's why I'm asking if we've tapped all other potential avenues."

We are clearly talking in circles. "Again, Alex, I'm open to any investors you bring to the table," I say in a tone that's slightly more friendly than J's was. "Our only angle right now is this strategic group of investors who clearly understands our vision. Our market test stated that we need to sell our product to consumers before businesses will buy it." Alex has always hated this idea, I know. I understand—it wasn't the original plan. But that's where we are now, though. Why are we rehashing all of this?

Our salads arrive, as do our drinks. Silence ensues. This isn't going well. This was not what J and I had in mind when we decided to take a detour and visit Alex. Wow, what a mistake! We could have skipped this lunch altogether and just headed to Napa to start our wine tasting.

Alex resumes speaking. "Maybe we're all too old—we just don't have the energy level that we had in our 20s."

What is he talking about? I wonder. J and I are looking at each other. *Is he trying to say that we haven't worked hard enough? Is "energy level" code for something?* We're two women who've dedicated our entire lives to this company… and he's going there.

J starts talking before I can open my mouth. "This has nothing to do with our 'energy levels,' Alex—we've tried so many avenues, but you didn't want to spend any more money, and we can't market the product without money." She leaves it at that. I have nothing more to add.

We're all trying not to end our lunch on a sour note; everyone is looking around and obviously trying to think of how to tactfully change the subject.

"So… where are you girls headed next?" Alex finally says.

"Calistoga to do a wine tasting," I say.

"Ahhh… that's nice."

Awkward!! We quickly eat our salads. Time to get out of here! Everybody's back in the campervan. As I climb back into the driver's seat, I take a real good inhale to smell the van and realize that it's downright nasty. We've got to air this out soon.

I look at Alex and smile in the hope that again he's not smelling what I'm smelling. He smiles back. There isn't much conversation on the way back to his house.

We pull up in his driveway and thank Alex for lunch and the use of his shower. We'll be in touch if anything new arises, we assure him.

He waves goodbye as I back out of his long driveway. J is still in the back on the sofa with Stormy; the passenger seat is empty. "That was a cluster," she says from behind me.

"I agree!" I say, nodding even though she can't see me. "At least the shower was good," I add. I quickly pull onto the main road. "Let's go to wine country!"

Chapter 16

Mud Bath

WE HAVE A two-and-a-half-hour drive to Calistoga. I can't wait to get to Napa Valley! J already reserved our next home base at a residential campsite that's surrounded by wineries. It sounds really nice! She's also got spa reservations for us tomorrow that will include taking mud baths and getting massages.

The drive is taking us through Napa, Yountville and St. Helena on Hwy 29. It's a great ride, with beautiful wineries lining both sides of the road. By the time we get into Calistoga, though, the sun has set. We spot a little market on Lincoln Boulevard, so we stop and buy a bottle of rosé for J and a pinot noir for me. That should last us for the next couple of days. I see a laundromat near the market. Pointing to it, I say to J, "We need to wash our clothes soon!"

The drive takes us farther north on Hwy 29. The two-lane road is pitch-dark, and we cannot see anything, not even the road signs (unless we're only about two feet away). I put on the brights since no cars are in front of us, and J navigates for us with her Waze app. Even with her assistance, I have to slow down to twenty-five miles per hour and squint at the road names to make sure we're where we want to be. We make a couple of turns off Hwy 29, driving over rocky, bumpy dirt roads. Finally, she sees the house number we're looking for.

We turn into the driveway and park the campervan next to a large oak tree that's beside a wire fence. The homeowners are not home during this time of year, I'm told by J—it'll just be us. It's eerily quiet, with the only light coming from the interior of the van and its exterior fog lights. When I get out, I hear crickets. It's kinda nice.

I grab Stormy and J leashes Striker. This time, along with our usual dog accessories, we strap on our headlamps. Because it's so dark even with the lamps, though, we only go for a short walk and don't stray far from the campervan. The landowner's house sits right in the middle of the property, an old-fashioned ranch with a large picture window that faces the backyard where we've parked. Apparently, there are a lot of interesting smells here, especially the ones coming from the vineyards—both dogs are bouncing off of the trees and plants. They haven't been this engaged with their environment since Yosemite.

We return to the van and start our routines: J lays out the rattan rug and the doggie beds along the side of the campervan and begins preparing dinner for the dogs as I set up my tent. Putting up a tent in the dark is much, much harder, I rediscover. It's been a long time since I've done this at night. With headlamp on, I lay out my tent frames, tent fly and tent stakes, and get the tent set up under the tree, right next to the side of the campervan. I then retrieve my tent lamp and place it on the rug, so we'll have some illumination for dinner.

The dogs are fed, and now it's our turn. I head to the van's kitchen and pull out the ingredients to make gluten-free spaghetti with tomato sauce, fresh basil and mozzarella cheese. It's a quick dinner to make— just ten minutes of prep and a fifteen-minute cooking time. J opens the bottle of pinot and we sip our wine as I drain the cooked spaghetti and toss everything together in a skillet.

I spoon the spaghetti into two small acrylic bowls and take it outside to the camper chairs, where J has placed our small cups of wine in the cup holders. The dogs are on their outside doggie beds, quietly monitoring our movements. We look around and its pitch-dark with the exception of the van's interior lights and the tent lamp.

Our simple dinner is good, and as we eat, we talk about Antonio having a fiancée, J's many admirers from the reunion last night and our conversation with Alex. All of this makes for a fun night of unfiltered girl talk filled with laughter and giggles. At times, our giggling gets uncontrollable; we thank the wine for its assistance with that. The dogs maintain a calm demeanor throughout the evening, and we thank them, too.

After we've tired ourselves out, I crawl into my tent and the dogs climb into the campervan with J. The night is still. We await the sunrise so that we can see our surroundings!

————————

Daylight penetrates the tent. It's bright! When I unzip the fly and peek out, I'm in awe—the vineyards are just a few feet away from me. I put on my hiking boots and scramble out of the tent. What a marvelous sight! I jump up and down with excitement. Time to get the dogs out to share this gorgeous countryside!

I slide open the van door to find Stormy waiting for me. "Are you up?" I whisper.

"Yes," J says from the back.

"Have you looked outside?" I shout. "It's amazing!"

She sits up, Striker still asleep on her legs, and pulls aside the curtain to peek outside. "Holy cow!" she blurts out.

I grab Stormy's leash and help him onto the step and out of the van. We begin by just walking around the house, but soon, we head to the dirt road we must have driven along last night. It's a dusty road lined with sprawling vineyards on both sides. The vines are flowering this time of year—the buds are opening, making the scenery magical. Napa Valley couldn't look more spectacular! We keep walking for about a mile, seeing stone winery buildings in the midst of the vineyards. A pickup truck goes by, showering both Stormy and me with dust. I wave hello to the driver. Who cares about dust when the scenery is so gorgeous?

We walk back to the campervan in all its red glory. Next to it, my blue tent is a pop of contrasting color. J is strolling with Striker, who's hopping along with lots of morning fervor. As Stormy and I approach her, we look at each other with the biggest smiles. "Isn't this something?" she exclaims. I tell her she couldn't have selected a better site. The views, the smells, the isolation, the proximity to the center of Calistoga with its spas and wineries… it's perfect!

Our spa day will begin at noon with mud baths, and J's been thinking of what to do with the dogs. It's too hot to just leave them in the campervan, so she gets on a dog-sitting app and starts looking for someone nearby who can dog-sit for a few hours while we're at the spa. As she's researching potential dog-sitters,

I'm googling "best coffee shop in Calistoga." There! I've found one: Calistoga Roastery, right on Lincoln Avenue. That sounds ideal.

She reads off a profile to me: she found a dog-sitter who's in his late 70s and lives in a small house right off of Lincoln Avenue and has a small backyard. Not surprisingly, he says that he loves dogs. We nod yes at the same time. "That works!" we both say. We'll head there as soon as we grab our coffees. His house is only a ten-minute drive from where we're located. So far, everything is working out perfectly for the day.

We have about an hour before we'll leave, so J lays out her yoga mat and starts to do sun salutations behind the van. The dogs are tied to the awning poles on the side, relaxing as I organize and tidy up a few things in my tent. I have both side vestibules and the storm flaps up, providing a fantastic window of the outdoors. The dogs are peacefully laid on their doggie beds enjoying the vineyards surrounding us, J is practicing her yoga and I have a stunning view. We are all happy campers at the moment.

Soon, it's time to get going, and everyone jumps into the van. We depart our campsite with the tent still up and the rugs and chairs in place for our return. It's a short drive into town on Hwy 29 south. As we enter downtown, I decide that Calistoga is my kind of place. It's charming, with streets lined with buildings from the early 1900s, and it has an unpretentious, small-town ambiance. It's also filled with small shops, cafés and restaurants. In one word, I would describe Calistoga as "cute," with her neighbors to the south, Yountville and St. Helena, being her gorgeously upscale sisters. The adjoining streets are filled with sweet, small, craftsman-style bungalows that make you think, *I could live here…*

I stop at the coffee shop and get our coffees and a breakfast pastry for J. The morning sun is warm, and there's not a cloud in the sky. The weather forecast says the temperature will be in the eighties. What a delightful spring day! We drink our coffees sitting outside the shop on a bench that faces Lincoln Avenue and just watch people walk, drive and cycle by. (*No scooters*, I think to myself.) It seems like time ticks by at a slower pace here, making for a lovely feeling of comfort and relaxation. Maybe the nearby underground hot springs are contributing to the blissed-out vibe. Even the dogs have a relaxed air about them this morning—they're more at ease now than they have been for the entire trip. Not even other dogs walking by are causing them to stir. I feel like we're sitting on a porch on a backcountry farm.

The dog-sitter's house is only a couple of blocks off the main road. We finish our coffees, get back into the campervan, find his house and park right in front. Like all of the other houses nearby, his is a small bungalow, although his is painted yellow and white and has a wooden side gate. We walk the dogs through the gate and into the backyard and knock on the back door.

"Hello, there!" we hear as the door is opened. A medium-size burly man steps outside and introduces himself as Mike. He immediately starts petting Striker and Stormy. He's a jolly-looking man with gray hair and a gray beard who makes me think of a kindly grandpa. He starts asking a lot of good questions about Striker's leg injury and his demeanor as well as Stormy's age and personality. All are excellent questions and prove that he's been around enough dogs to sense their attitudes and what he can expect once we leave.

J is comfortable leaving them with him, so much so that she asks if we could leave them there for the entire day. "Of course," he says. "Enjoy the day and don't worry about the dogs—they'll be fine."

I give him a grateful look. I just love this man! He can tell that we need a doggie break. "We'll pick them back up after dinner," says J.

For the first time in I don't know how many days—it feels like weeks—we are without the dogs. It's a bit freeing!

The spa where J has reserved our mud baths is about a mile away. Once we're in the parking lot, we pull out our small bags and stuff them with a change of clothes, toiletries and swimsuits. We are ready to just relax! We check in, and pretty soon, they call our names and lead us to the women's locker room so that we can change into terrycloth robes. After that, we head to the lounge to wait for our attendants. I'm already beginning to feel that relaxed spa sensation, and we haven't even started. When they call our names again, we're led to a back room for a quick shower before going into a room with large stone tubs filled with black mud. The air is thick with steam.

Wow! I've never seen anything like this before. I did take a mud bath in Turkey once, but not in a spa—I was lathered in mud next to a river and asked to lie on nearby rocks so that the sun could dry out the mud. Later, my fellow bathers and I were hosed down with warm water to remove the caked-on mud. It was a bit provincial, but I will say that my skin was silky-soft for days. This experience, though, will be totally different. Given its proximity to volcanic ash deposits and thermal hot springs, Calistoga is the mud bath capital of California. Judging by everything J has read, this is promising to be good!

In the mud room, my spa attendant asks me to sit at the edge of the stone tub and slowly slide into the mud mixture. It's hot! Seconds later, my entire body is floating on a weightless mixture that feels like a form-fitting, wet, gooey blanket. She covers my fore-head with a cool, wet towel. Except for my forehead, my entire body feels warm and wonderful. I can barely hear J next to me—I'm in my own world. I close my eyes and relax. When the attendant asks how it feels,

I can only moan, "Nice…Really nice…" I can already feel the toxins leaving my body and the relief in my leg and shoulder muscles.

After fifteen minutes, the attendants move both J and me to the showers to remove the mud. Next is a hot mineral bath, where again we soak with our eyes closed and topped with cucumber slices. Then it's off to the steam room for a few minutes. Finally, we go our separate ways and an attendant takes me to a small room, where she has me lie down and then wraps my body to begin the cool-down.

What an experience! I'm exhausted. I'm lying on a small spa bed when I'm called to move to yet another lounge area. I change into my terrycloth robe (my hair is wrapped into a towel) and grab the cucumber water. The attendants had said it's important to drink lots of water while we're here, so I happily chug away. J comes out and sits on the chair next to me. She tells me that my face is glowing.

"I feel like a shiny new penny," I say. "You're also aglow." And there's more to come, too—now it's time for our massages.

When my name is called, I'm introduced to my masseuse, Hector. He leads me to a back room where I take off my robe and lie face-up under a warm set of blankets. He begins the massage. For me, though, the problem with massages is that they've never really been too relaxing, because I keep following where the masseuse's hand is going and am concerned it could get a little too close to my private areas. That means I can't totally relax.

Afterwards, I head to another beautiful lounge on the property. J is already there. We both look wiped, but in a good way. I ask her how her massage was, and she says she doesn't remember much because she fell asleep. "Fell asleep?" I echo. There's no way I could sleep with some guy running his hands all over my body!

We're asked if we want to use the pool for the day. "Hell, yes!" we answer. Good thing we brought our swimsuits. We change into them and decide to grab a salad at the pool bar and find a couple of lounge chairs. This is turning out to be a really good day. *Was it really only a couple of days ago that we were in Yosemite?* I think. *Feels like ages… so much has happened between Half Dome and today.* We spend the rest of the afternoon in and out of the thermal pool with a few glasses of chardonnay.

J asks if I think the dogs are all right. I nod. "Yes, there's no need to worry—'Uncle Mike' has it all under control." She seems satisfied with my answer.

It's getting late in the afternoon—shade has overtaken the entire pool area. Time for an early dinner before picking up the dogs. I google "best restaurants in Calistoga" and quickly scroll through the reviews. "Evangeline sounds perfect for tonight," I tell J. "They have a garden patio, and it's right around the corner."

What would we do without Google? I'm trying to think back to how I traveled before… *Ah, yes, there were Lonely Planet books. Or you found out things by talking with the locals and other tourists.*

We walk over to Evangeline and find that the patio is perfect—it's so pretty, so California, so wine-country, so relaxed and cozy. Unfortunately, there are no tables available because we don't have reservations. We can sit at the bar and eat, though, which better suits our style, anyway.

For some reason, I'm in the mood for champagne; J orders the same. We're sitting next to a lovely couple from Chicago. I love sitting at bars and being able to talk to people! We tell the couple about our journey thus far. They're quite intrigued, and at the end of the night, they pick up the tab for us all. Just another wonderful example of how meeting strangers while traveling is as much fun as the places themselves. It just enriches the entire experience. How fortunate that there were no tables available on the patio!

With dinner finished, it's time to retrieve the dogs. We drive back to Mike's house, open the side gate and go to the back. We can hear Striker barking from inside the house. The door opens and there he is, tail wagging feverishly. He jumps up on J as Stormy is right behind him, waiting for Striker to get out of the way. I reach down to grab Stormy. Mike says both dogs were good, but Striker kept looking out of the window for J to come back. "Definitely some separation issues with him," he says. *Yup.*

J thanks Mike for everything and we get back into the van and head to the campsite. Instead of joining me up front, J sits in the back with Striker—he's still anxious and wanting to be next to her.

Another superb day! And to top it off, Mike already fed the dogs, so we don't have doggie dinner duty tonight. After a quick walk around the property with our headlamps on, everybody is ready to turn in for the night.

Chapter 17

Wine Tasting

J's *FORMER COLLEGE* roommate, Sally, lives near Santa Rosa, so prior to finalizing our travel plans, J contacted her and asked if she wanted to join us for a wine tasting. She said yes and that she would be happy to organize an itinerary near where we'd be staying in Calistoga, along the Silverado Trail. Seeing as she lives in Sonoma County, and works in the hospitality field, she's up-to-date on all of the best wineries, even the smaller ones that not many people know about. She'll be a great resource to help us figure out where to go. I'm happy to leave it all in her hands.

After our morning routine of feeding and walking the dogs, J and I are relaxing on the camp chairs, looking out at the rolling vineyards and discussing what to do with the dogs today. My suggestion is to take them back to Mike, but she thinks it might be too much for

Striker to be away from her for two consecutive days and suggests that we go wine tasting together.

"Wine tasting *together*?" I say in disbelief. "All of us?"

"They can stay in the van," she offers. But the weather report indicates it's going to be over eighty degrees today! I briefly cover my face with my hands as I try to picture the scene. We're taking the campervan? I don't know why, but I somehow thought J would have planned a wine tasting day without the dogs and maybe even without the campervan. I can't hide my this-is-a-dumb-idea expression. I think I need my almond milk latte, but there are only two ways I'm going to get the coffee I need very badly right now: either I go and J stays with the dogs, or we all go together. J wants a macchiato, too, so everybody gets in the van. It's a mini road trip just to get coffee, but fortunately, we manage it rather quickly this time. Somehow.

When we return to the campsite, Sally is there waiting for us. She gets out of her car and throws her arms around J. They haven't seen each other in over a decade, I remember. They give each other big bear hugs, and then J introduces me, the dogs and Kojak the campervan.

"Wow!" Sally says as she peers inside the van. "This is so awesome. What an amazing trip! I must come with you guys next time." She's a tall 50-something woman herself, with long legs and long, curly blonde hair. She's also an energetic ball of fire and excited about all the wineries she's planned for us to visit today. Apparently, she's been working on this for weeks. I'm impressed! *Wait til she hears that the dogs are joining!*

She sees Striker's leg and asks what happened. J answers with the canned response: "He jumped out of my second-story balcony, had surgery and is doing really well now." As she's answering, J looks at me and smiles. Yes, we've now repeated this story over a hundred times.

Sally kneels down to pet Striker and Stormy. "Where are you guys going today?" she asks them. I eagerly await J's answer.

"I was thinking of taking them with us," J says. "They can stay in the van."

Sally looks at me questioningly. *Yes*, I think, *I'm guessing that isn't what you had in mind, either.*

A few seconds of silence pass before Sally says, "Oh… okay… well, yeah."

Sally's cool—I like her. She's going with the flow. I'm sure she's frantically re-planning her schedule already.

We all pile into the van. Sally is in the passenger seat next to me and J's on the sofa between Striker and Stormy. Both dogs are quiet at the moment, but Stormy clearly is not happy to be sharing the sofa with Striker.

Our first stop is about twenty minutes away. Seeing as I'm the designated driver, I'm going to go light on the wine tasting… Maybe I'll just stay with reds.

We're driving along on Silverado Trail Boulevard. It's a scenic, two-lane highway on the eastern edge of Napa Valley. There's a bike lane for cyclists to the right, and everywhere there are spectacular, endless rolling vineyards as far as the eye can see. Since it's Sunday, plenty of cyclists are on the road, so the drive is a little slower. That's fine, though—this way, we have time to truly enjoy the countryside in all its grandeur.

Sally is navigating. She directs me to turn into our first winery, Clos Pegase. What an entrance! I'm surprised to see such a modern, stately building, but it's beautiful nonetheless. As we park, J suggests we take the dogs for a quick walk before we start tasting. We pull out the dog accessories while Sally looks on, and then J and I walk them along the perfectly manicured grounds for about fifteen minutes. When we return them to the van, we leave the windows half-down and the van fan on. J slides the door shut and takes a big breath. "Do you think they'll be okay?"

"Yes, but we can also see if dogs are allowed on the patio," I say.

"Let's go!" says Sally. She's anxious to get started.

We're warmly welcomed at the stunning entrance. No reservations are required to taste—we're skipping the tours and going straight to wine tasting. We have a lot of vineyards to cover!

We're escorted to the patio overlooking the beautiful rows and rows of vineyards. *Thank you, Sally!* I think. J immediately tells the story of her two dogs, one aging, the other injured, asking if dogs are permitted to be with us on the patio, and is thrilled when she's told, "Yes." She goes back to the van and gets both dogs. They're clearly elated to join us. Stormy calmly lies down beside J while Striker keeps trying to get onto her lap. She's trying hard to keep him down. It's not working.

The waiter gives us a nice overview of all the wines on the menu. J and Sally order the winery's classic flight, beginning with whites and moving to reds. I'm sticking with the reds: a flight of syrah, pinot noir and cabernet sauvignon. We're all hungry, too, so we request a nice cheeseboard and ask them to recommend what might work best.

"Oh, this is so much fun!" Sally blurts out.

We all clap like little girls. "Yes, it is!" I say. We take a quick selfie of us three. Then we take another of us five.

The wines arrive along with the cheeseboard, and we say "Cheers!" to Sally for planning this glorious day for us. We clink our glasses and begin the tasting. Superb, just superb, all the wines and pairings…J and

Sally rave about the rosé and chardonnay. Could any other winery match this place? I could sit here and keep drinking reds all day, but we have more to experience and taste, so we thank the staff for allowing us to have the dogs on the patio and I buy a bottle of chardonnay for J and a pinot noir for me. Off to our second stop!

We navigate back to Silverado Trail and head to Quixote, a small winery at the end of a long, private road where Sally has made a reservation for a tasting. Again, we ask if dogs are permitted on the patio, and again we are pleasantly surprised with a "Yes." It's a very dog-friendly environment in Napa!

Compared to other wineries in the area, Quixote's estate is whimsical, colorful and unique. It's smaller than most Napa Valley wineries, too, and its unorthodox design, style and layout imbue it with a special sense of discovery. Again, we're warmly welcomed at the front by the winery hostess manager and then escorted to the patio, which has a grand view of the property's vineyards and the hills beyond, which are sprinkled with lavender and stunning olive trees. What a sight!

I'm looking forward to more reds. J and Sally also go with reds, so that makes red flights all around. The syrah and cabernet sauvignon are outstanding: deep, rich and bold. I can't go into all of the descriptive adjectives, suffice to say, it's so damn good. At this second winery, both dogs are chilled, quietly lying on the uneven tile floors next to us, also appreciating the scenery. Who wouldn't? It's nice to see them sit idly as we enjoy our wine tasting. By now, I've reached my limit of what I can safely drink given that I'm the designated driver. I purchase bottles of the syrah and cab and a couple of souvenir acrylic wine glasses. We're off to our third and final winery to visit based on Sally's excellent itinerary.

It doesn't take long to get to Chateau Montana. Whoa! Another exceptional property. Once you visit these vineyards and see the charm, love and care that goes into them and then taste the wines they produce, it's no surprise that Napa is known as the wine capital of the U.S. We take the dogs for another quick walk and approach the entrance to ask if we could do a tasting where dogs are allowed.

The hostess manager welcomes us and the dogs, petting Striker and Stormy in turn before leading us to the patio. I see more of the spectacular, majestic sights we've been viewing all day. Even though it's our third winery visit, I just can't get accustomed to these splendid views—endless, lush vineyards as far as the eye can see! Like the other properties in Napa, reds are the stars on the menu here, too, but J and Sally decide to go with whites. I'm passing since I'm driving. The dogs are looking around and enjoying their surroundings. I think they sense how extraordinary this place is and are happy to be a part of our experience.

After three wineries, all of us are done. Back at the campsite, everyone gets out and we secure the dogs. I'm ready to start dinner—we're all starving! Tasting has given us large appetites. We invite Sally to join us tonight, and seeing as she's been drinking, we recommend she should sleep here, too. She agrees and calls her husband to let him know she's staying with us and will drive back early tomorrow morning. Yay, we have a guest for dinner! Fantastic.

I tell Sally that we're only eating veggies on this trip, and she's good with that. I lay out two large picnic tablecloths on the ground to make a big blanket, aka our dinner table. It's starting to get dark now, so I add my tent lamp and table lamp to the blanket/table, giving our dining area a nice ambience. J and Sally take the dogs for a walk while I prep and assemble dinner. Bonus: J has figured out our outdoor audio system, and since we're all alone on the property, we can play our music loudly. The Lumineers, John Mayer, Radiohead, The xx and Coldplay are now booming through the van's speakers.

Dinner includes guac and chips, corn avocado salad and veggie quesadillas. J and Sally arrange the dinnerware, plates of food and wine glasses on our "dinner table." We're opening one of the bottles we tasted earlier today, a pinot noir. We sit on the blanket, raise our acrylic wine glasses and say, "Here's to a great day and great friends!" and dig into dinner. After we've eaten and had more wine, we turn up the music. Why not? We've got the place to ourselves, and obviously, we're all tipsy. We start dancing. Even Striker with his three-and-a-half legs joins in.

Tonight, it's three girls, two dogs and a campervan.

Chapter 18

Big Sur

*T*HE NEXT MORNING dawns brightly again. We all went to sleep rather late last night, drinking wine, dancing and talking late into the night. The last I remember, as I zipped shut my tent, the others were piling into the campervan, but I have no idea who ended up sleeping where. I take a few minutes to enjoy the stillness and the birds chirping while I look up at the brightly illuminated tent overhead. We're leaving wine country today—Big Sur will be our next and final stop.

I start to hear some commotion: doors opening, van door sliding and voices speaking, first Sally's voice and then J's. I unzip the panel flaps and peer out at the van. The girls and the dogs are just stepping outside. "Good morning!" I call out. "How did everyone sleep?"

"Not too well," says a disheveled Sally with a half-smile. As she exits the van, she stumbles out, almost missing the step. Quite frankly, she looks like a mini-tornado hit her. She didn't have to tell me she didn't sleep—it's pretty much reflected all over her face. Messy tangled hair, smeared mascara and puffy eyes… Poor thing. "Do you want coffee or tea?" I ask.

"No, No. I've got to get going," she quickly shouts out. She is so ready to leave.

"Stormy moved around a bunch," J adds. That's code for "the dogs didn't want anything or anyone trespassing on their regular spots." They must have been naughty.

"It was wonderful to hang out with you both!" Sally says graciously. "Thanks so much for reaching out!" She gives J a big hug, then comes over to me with her arms open and gives me a big hug as well. She's got to get home, shower and head to work, she tells us, so she needs to leave now (it's 6:30 a.m.) to beat some of the traffic. She gets in her car and drives off, waving once more.

"That was fun!" J says, smiling.

I agree. "She's a great girl!" I go over to J and put my arm around her as we both wave goodbye to Sally. "How bad was it to sleep?"

J sighs. "Stormy and Striker didn't want to share their areas—dogs have their routines. She was a trooper, though."

I nod. *It all looks so easy from the outside,* I think.

Now time for our usual morning drill of walking the dogs, feeding them breakfast and breaking down our camp. We punctuate our chores with light chatter this morning, still reeling a bit from all of last night's wine. It's going to take a few hours and some coffee to get the cobwebs out…

Our second camp is now history: the tent, camp chairs and rattan rug are all thrown into the carriage cart in the back, and the awning is rolled. As J completes her doggie duties, I'm reviewing what needs to be done before we get back on the road. We have very little sink water left, for one thing, so we'll need to find a dump station to replenish our water tanks and dispose of the gray and black water. I google "dump stations near me," and a list of stations within a few miles appears. Second, we need to refill the gas tank. Third, we need to do laundry! Our clothes downright stink. *Hold up! First, I need coffee,* I remind myself.

"Let's put in a load of laundry while we have our coffees," I suggest to J. "The laundromat is only a couple of blocks from the coffee shop."

"Great idea!" she says.

We all hop into the campervan and say goodbye to our wonderful campsite. I drive into town and pull into the laundromat's parking lot, then grab my backpack as J grabs her suitcase. Stormy stays in the van on his sofa seat, but J brings along Striker since he's jumpy this morning. Happily, we're the only ones in the laundromat at this hour. We dump all of our clothes into two large loads, one dark and one white (including towels). "I can't wait to have clean clothes again!" I exclaim.

I head to the coin machine to get change for the machines and see a bulletin board above it. A flyer for a music festival catches my attention. "BottleRock in Napa Valley," it reads. That sounds fantastic! I'm a huge music festival lover. Whoever invented the concept of these festivals should be sainted. If it were any other time, I'd go.

We go back to the van and get Stormy for our walk over to the coffee shop. While J keeps an eye on the dogs outside, I go in, order my almond milk latte and her macchiato and bring them out for us to drink. We sit on the bench and silently survey the main road. We really enjoyed Calistoga's vibe, its ease and especially the dog-friendly campsite.

I look over at J and say, "There's a music festival in Napa today."

"There is?" she asks with interest. "That would be fun."

"Yes, and Muse is headlining it tonight. I love Muse," I say enthusiastically.

"But what would we do with the dogs? Could we take them with us?" she asks.

I shake my head. "No, no, no pets allowed in music

festivals." We survey the scene silently again. *I'd love to go,* I'm thinking. *But we would need to find a doggie sitter… another Mike, except one in Napa, which is twenty-five miles away. Plus, we'd need to revise our Big Sur campsite reservations and the return date of the campervan…*

We start talking about the logistics of the idea, but after a great deal of deliberation, we conclude it would be too much trouble to change our plans at this point. Darn.

After our coffees, we return to the laundromat, move our clothes into the dryer, wait for them to dry and then fold them and pile them into neat stacks. Our clothes are clean and smell good. What a relief! There's nothing like clean clothes.

I go out to the van to retrieve our bags so that we can quickly pack, but before I can get back to the laundromat, Striker has jumped up and attacked our stacks. Our clean clothes are now strewn all over the dirty floor.

I look over at J and shake my head at Striker. "Why?" I say, staring down at him with a stern look.

"Well, at least they still smell good," she says with a laugh. We pick up our clothes, shake off the dirt and just throw them into our bags. "Forget folding them," I say. "Let's go."

When we get back into the van and the dogs are back in their usual spots, I say sidelong to J, "Do you think Striker overheard us talking about leaving him again and he retaliated by going after our clothes?"

She can only look at him on the bed and shrug. Doggie Mystery!

———————

We find the dump station. J puts on her latex gloves, opens the compartment with the hose and extends it into the station's hole. She opens the valve knob and begins the procedure of emptying the tanks. Boy, she's good at this. When she's done with that, I start filling the water tanks on the other side of the van. We're so proud of ourselves as we get back into the van. High-five! Once again, we nailed this unattractive but necessary task. Next, it's to the gas station to fill up our gas tank.

We are finally off! Our road trip has officially now resumed. I've got my playlist on and am looking forward to our next destination, Big Sur. Road trips provide such a gleeful sense of "What's next?" and "We're moving on!"

The Waze app clocks the route at almost four hours. While on Route 101, we decide we'll stop in Carmel to have lunch and give the dogs a break. The morning traffic is typical, but as we continue on the 101, it clears as we drive farther south. Once we're on Hwy 1, though, there's construction as we approach Carmel. Slowing down, we exit into town. I love Carmel! It's a northern California coastal town that oozes casual refinement along with subtle beach sophistication. We park near the beach, grab the doggie accessories and start our walk. The air is chilly, with temps back in the fifties. It's a big change from Calistoga, which was in the mid-seventies when we left this morning. It's quite windy here, too, but the dogs are appreciating the ocean air as it starts to blow in their doggie faces.

We stroll down to the sand where there's a very small crowd. Both Striker and Stormy are moving vigorously along. It's getting hard to keep up with Stormy! J says, "Unleash him and let him go."

"Really?" I say. I've never heard her say that before, but I'm happy to do so. When I unleash him, Stormy takes off like a jaguar, sprinting along the beach like a young lad. Where did this come from? Now he sees other dogs ahead and J's getting worried, so we all run after him, including Striker, who's hopping along, still leashed to J.

"Stormy! Stormy!" we scream at the top of our lungs. "Stormy, come here!" He's deaf, but something made him stop and he looks at us like we're two crazy girls (and I swear I can see him smiling) and then runs the other way. There are other unleashed dogs, and they all seem to bounce into each other and start to play.

We continue to run and Striker continues to hop along on his three-and-a-half legs for another 200 yards, finally catching up to Stormy as he starts to slow his pace (*finally*). I hook his leash back into his collar and the four of us walk slowly back, out of breath. There's so much slobber coming out of Stormy's mouth, it's gushing of spit. But, what a workout! Now the ocean air feels even better against all our faces!

We find the nearest café that allows dogs on the patio. We're exhausted; chasing Stormy has tired us all. I look down at him— he's back to his "grandpa" personality and I glare deep into his eyes. Where did that energy come from? What a transformation!

We have a quick bite and refresh the dogs with lots of water and a few treats. The walk back to the van is painfully slow for Stormy, but he makes it. We're back on the road.

The twenty-six-mile drive from Carmel to Big Sur is iconic—it's one of the most dramatic, breathtaking, memorable drives in the world, with steep, rugged cliffs on the left and the Pacific Ocean pounding against rocks on the right. We've both been here before, but the view never gets old. The only drawback is that today is a bit overcast, with lots of gray clouds blocking the sun that stubbornly keeps trying to peek out. It's a two-lane winding road that leads just north of Big Sur.

There sits the Bixby Creek Bridge, one of the most photographed spots on the planet. J and I get out and take quite a few photos. We keep the dogs in the van, though—we don't want to risk any further potential chases or mishaps. Fortunately, the beach walk/run/chase made them both very tired, and they are content to stay behind.

Dozens and dozens of other tourists are taking photos. As I look out at the sweeping view, one word describes what's before me: "amazing." This sight should be on everybody's must-see list. Although we are finished with our picture-taking, I just do not want to leave.

As was the case with Half Dome, I just want to pause here. It's important to appreciate where you are, and then lock in everything you're feeling and all of the sensations that are coming over you. I rest my eyes on this moment and this memory. It's a meditation of seizing the moment; I'm as present as I've ever been. I close my eyes, smell the salt-water air and feel the sea wind blowing against my face and body. A big inhale and a big exhale… and I open my eyes.

I look over at J and say, "We are so lucky."

She nods. "I know."

A few more deep breaths and long moments of staring at the blue waters below, and then we head back to the van, where the dogs are asleep—the sandy beach and fresh air exhausted them to a state of happy unconsciousness. *Sleeping doggies are a good thing*, I think. We have a few more miles to drive on Hwy 1 before we reach Pfeiffer Big Sur State Park campground, which sits on the mountain side of the highway. J tried to get us into the campgrounds on the beachside but no dogs are allowed. Bummer!

When we get to our campsite, we see that it's larger than what we had at Yosemite, with more space between the individual campsites. Each is also completely surrounded by redwood trees of all shapes and sizes. No other campers are near us, and it's really quiet. Maybe it's still a little early. The set-up goes smoothly: tent, chairs, rug, awning, picnic table. (We truly are pros now.) Soon, the dogs are ready for their walks, and although they're tired from earlier today, their smelling senses are once again heightened. Nature is back!

Striker's hopping along in and out of the brush and around the trees. Stormy's going along at a much slower pace, but he's still very interested in what's around him. They're not letting this opportunity go to waste even if they are tired—it's too appealing for that! After forty-five minutes, we arrive back to the campsite. It's almost dusk, so J starts the campfire. It's getting colder, too.

I uncork a bottle of sauvignon blanc from yesterday's wine-tasting, along with some cheese, crackers and crudités (assorted raw veggies) with an artichoke dip. We start our happy hour. *Another great concept— who invented happy hour?* I think.

It's such a satisfying, basic way of traveling to be within nature, sharing a meal and camping. And, in this particular case, we're set amongst some of the oldest trees in the world. It's so incredibly balancing and rewarding! Ahhh…the simple life really is the best life.

As we watch darkness come upon us, we see more campers drive up and start setting up their campsites. J adds more logs to our campfire, ahhh, the smell of a campfire, I just love that smell and the sound of crackling wood burning. I start preparing dinner. Tonight, it's a vegetable frittata, made with sweet peppers and onions and a chopped kale salad. This little kitchenette has proven to be a treasure.

With our table lamp providing us perfect dinner lighting, we enjoy our meal out on the picnic table, along with our wine, and then call it an early night— we have a long day planned tomorrow, and I want to hit the hiking trails early.

Chapter 19

Midnight

'M SLOWLY AWAKENED by chilly weather and loudly chirping birds. The sun has risen, but due to the tall redwood trees surrounding our campsite, we can't see it. It's really peaceful…I feel a calm serenity coming over me this morning. It must be these soaring trees and the isolation of not having any neighbors adjoining our campsite. J is up early, so we all go for our morning dog walk together. As we did at Yosemite, we're back to putting on our knit caps, scarves, gloves and fleece jackets.

We walk along the paved road, allowing the dogs to slightly veer off into the brush and trees. They're competing to see which tree or brush to smell next, pushing against each other as to who gets to mark it first. Because Striker is still hopping on three-and-a-half legs, he bounces around with an open back leg and at times winds up spraying Stormy. It's my job to watch out for that spray and to pull Stormy away when I see Striker taking aim.

That special spring in their step both dogs had at Yosemite is back in their paces. They've got their tongues out and are wagging their tails and are obviously in sheer joy. Even with Stormy's age and Striker's disability, their energy levels have soared new heights on this road trip, especially when we're in parks.

After the walk and our breakfast, J and I talk through our plans for the day. She's been researching the local hot springs and has uncovered a really interesting find—visiting the Big Sur Esalen in the early morning hours. By early, I mean 1 a.m. The idea of experiencing the hot springs baths with or without our bathing suits and then soaking in a healing mineral tub for a few hours in the middle of the night atop cliffs above the Pacific Ocean sounds wildly bohemian! But reservations can only be made the day of and only online, and we have no signal at the campsite.

There is, however, a lodge a couple of miles away towards the entrance of the campgrounds, and I'm thrilled to discover that it also has a coffee shop. I can get my almond milk latte *and* make our reservations—perfect! J stays back with the dogs, preferring to relax at the campsite for the day. I'm sure she'll read and practice her yoga.

I arrive at the lodge, order my latte and reserve slots for us for tonight. We'll need to arrive just after midnight for our soaking time of 1 a.m. to 3 a.m. Hurray! Although it dawns on me: what are we going to do with the dogs? Are we going to the springs in the campervan? I'm hoping J has thought this through, but in any case, I've done my part by getting us in. I sit on the patio overlooking the redwood forest and a nearby creek and sip my latte. It's going to be another good day!

Starting from the lodge, I begin to tackle my first hike: Buzzard's Roost. I've read it's a three-mile-long moderate hiking trail along shady oak and redwood trees that will ascend steeply at the end and give me a panoramic view of the ocean. It sounds just right—it's enough to reinvigorate my hiking juices. But, uh-oh, at the trailhead, I see a posted warning: "Beware of mountain lions and don't hike alone."

Well, that's just great, I think. I see these "Don't hike alone" warnings often when I go hiking—it's not new. Given the bear sighting at Yosemite last week, though, I'm a little more conscious of the fact I may encounter one of these dangerous animals, and the warning does make me pause for just a second. I remember a recent news report of a solo woman hiker being attacked by a mountain lion; after that hit the headlines, of course, my family called to remind me of the danger of hiking alone. *But that's such a rare occurrence*, I tell myself. *I just need to stay focused on my surroundings. It sure would be a downer to end our trip with being mauled by a mountain lion!*

I march onward and soon see plenty of hikers. For the first time hiking solo, I consciously think about keeping other hikers in my view. The trail is narrow, but it's easy to follow, and the ascent is gradual. The shade from the forest makes the temperature quite pleasant. As I hike along, I keep encountering other hikers, and I hear lots of foreign languages, including French, German and what I presume is Russian.

After the final incline—this one is steep—I finally reach the summit and anxiously look out at the ocean. Bummer! The view is hidden by clouds, and I can't see the ocean. That's a bit disappointing. I decide to take a break before returning, so I sit down on a large rock and get out the banana and orange I brought with me. As other hikers approach the end of the trail, everyone has the same reaction I did: "Oh, no! I can't see anything!"

Overall, though, the trail was still worthwhile. Hiking through a forest of trees I have never experienced before makes the case that sometimes it is the journey and not the destination that really matters. The descent back to the lodge is easy, and along the way, I see another trail: Pfeiffer Falls and Valley View. It looks like it's short enough that I can have a go at this one as well—it's still early in the afternoon, and I have enough water in my bladder and snacks in my bag to keep going.

The beginning of this trail hits you with a large grove of redwoods on the banks of a small creek. This is the best part of the trail! I've never seen trees this large and stately. I know that this area (and most of Big Sur's trails) have recently been heavily damaged by fires, and as I gaze at this natural wonderland, I just hope and pray future generations will have the opportunity to experience this years from now.

The trail ascends quickly; the trees are now below and behind me. The hidden sun is still trying to peek out as I continue upwards along the trail. After the short climb to the summit, I'm rewarded with a clearer, partially sunny view of the valley canyon stretching all the way to the ocean. I pause to savor it, then head back down the same I came way up. This time, I slow down as I walk past the redwoods, look up, stop and spend time appreciating all their grandeur. I see a family of four coming up the trail and the father stops and educates his young daughter on the trees and surrounding life. What a beautiful moment. I love it when I see families together on trails.

Now that it's mid-afternoon, I start returning back to the campsite. Just as it had been at Yosemite, the van's bright-red presence makes it easy to spot from a quarter-mile away. I spot J sitting on a camp chair and Striker and Stormy lying on the rug looking out onto the park. They've all turned into such campers! As I get closer, I call out, and both dogs get up with their tails wagging, pushing forward as far as their leashes allow.

J's had a relaxing day: she read, practiced yoga, went for a cold swim in the shallow creek and walked the dogs a couple of times along the paved roadway within the park. I give her a short rundown of the hiking trails and tell her that we're all set for later tonight/early morning at Esalen. She's thrilled that we were able to get in. "What do you think about the dogs?" I ask her.

"I think the dogs will be fine in the van—it's cool enough at that time, and it's only a couple of hours," she replies.

I'm relieved. Given that we took the dogs with us to the wineries, I was prepared to hear that she wanted to bring them along to the springs as well. Though, I'm almost sure it's not allowed.

Seeing as we'll be heading out during the middle of the night, we decide it would be worthwhile to do a dry run now and take a quick jaunt to where the Esalen resort sits on Hwy 1. We all get into the campervan, drive out of Pfeiffer State Park and turn south towards Esalen. It's late afternoon, giving us plenty of sunlight to get good views of the surrounding area (which will no doubt be totally dark later tonight).

We park in the lot and walk down to the spring's hot tubs, leaving the dogs in the van. The late-emerging afternoon sun is already setting, and the view over-looking the Pacific Ocean at this hour is nothing short of magnificent, with endless crystal-blue, sparkling water. We are greeted by Esalen staff and let them know that we have reservations for later tonight. They show us where the shower rooms are and reiterate what we've read: whether or not we wear bathing suits is up to us. Most bathers do not. *What an experience this will be!* I think.

We head back to the campsite, where J leashes the dogs to the picnic table and starts the campfire. We're both eager for what's to come later tonight. She feeds the dogs while I prepare something to nibble on in the campervan. It's not long before we're sitting in the camp chairs under the awning having our wine and hummus and chips and discussing whether we should be naked in the tubs or put on our bathing suits. We agree: let's be naked.

Neither of us are too hungry—J's been snacking all day, and the hummus is enough for me. We forgo dinner and decide to get some sleep before getting up at 11:30 p.m. to leave for the springs. Hopefully we'll be able to sleep! We're both nearly jumping up and down with enthusiasm for our hot tubs appointment. We say "Goodnight!" knowing we'll see each other again in a few hours. I climb into my tent and J steps into the campervan with Striker and Stormy.

Four hours later, my alarm rings. I rub my eyes and turn my headlamp on, quickly changing into a couple of additional layers of clothing. I have a small backpack that I packed last night with my bathing suit (in case I change my mind), flip-flops and T-shirt. I open the tent fly and look out to see darkness that's only interrupted by the bright stars way above the trees. Going over to the van, I slide open the door.

"Are you ready?" I quietly whisper to J. She whispers back a yes. Stormy has opened his eyes, but he isn't moving, and even though Striker is stirring a bit in his crate, all seems quiet. Thank goodness.

I slide into the driver's seat and J scrambles into the passenger seat. We start to slowly drive out of the campgrounds as quietly as we can. (I know we're waking fellow campers by starting the engine.) We turn left onto Hwy 1—which is completely dark—and head south. Esalen is about thirty minutes away. As we enter the parking lot, we see a few other cars already there and waiting to get in.

As Striker sees his mommy moving around the interior of the van, he starts jumping around in his crate. J says, "Let's take them for a little walk before we go in—we're early, anyway."

I look over at Stormy and see that he's looking at me, wondering what's going on. "Why not?" I say. "Let's go."

We put on our headlamps, leash the dogs and get out of the van. In front of us and behind us, there's a line of cars waiting to get in, but we seem to be the only ones who brought along dogs. We give them a few minutes to do their business and then get them back into the van.

The other cars are moving along now. It's time! We make sure the dogs are comfortable and then head for the entrance with our backpacks in tow and our head-lamps on. It's a chilly night. We and the entire group of people who have been waiting are escorted quickly to the changing room. It's going to be a communal experience, apparently, yet no one is wearing a bathing suit. I'm a bit surprised—I had thought there would be one or two holdouts. *Are we surrounded by a bunch of hippies? Counter-culture freaks?* I wonder. *It's part of the adventure—no judgment.*

Once we change out of our clothes, we head down to one of the few sulfur-scented public tubs that are available at midnight. They're fueled by the local hot water springs nearby, and when we get in, the water is not only warm, it's downright hot. J looks over at me and says, "I can't believe how gorgeous this is! It's so nice." There's almost a full moon out and it's providing quite a sea view straight in front of us.

I nod. "I agree!" I look around at all the naked people getting into the tubs. "So far, so good—no weirdos here," I whisper. She smiles back.

The ocean below is surprisingly quiet. The sky is full of bright, twinkling stars. I'm not usually a late-night person, but I'm wide-awake now—this unparalleled view is mind-blowing! It's a stunning, serene setting, and thankfully, the other people in the tub with us are considerate and friendly. Just like us, they're blown away by what we're experiencing. I sit back and enjoy capturing another awe-inspiring moment.

J is engaged in small talk, and although I occasionally join in, honestly, I just want to sink into these springs and remain silent. The two hours fly by. Afterwards, we return to the shower room—the showers are another wonderful experience—and find our way back to the van. Stormy is sitting in the driver's seat, looking out over the steering wheel, waiting for us to come back. How on earth did he maneuver to the front? Sometimes the intentions and movements of these dogs are truly puzzling. Another, Doggie Mystery! But, I'm too tired to think about it any further tonight.

When we arrive back to our campsite at 3:30 a.m., we probably wake up several of our neighbors again. *I'm sorry!* I think as I park. I move out of the van and wish J goodnight before finding my way back to my tent and quickly rushing into my sleeping bag. My hair is damp and my body limp, and I'm asleep within minutes.

Chapter 20

Modest Mouse or Muse

CAN'T BELIEVE WE'RE going home today! I sit up in my tent and look around, tapping my tent floor with both hands. "Thank you for being such a good home for me!" I say aloud. With the late night we had, I'm pretty tired and not ready to get up yet. I open up the side panels to veer over at the campervan. Everything seems quiet, so I just let myself settle back down on my mat and slowly close my eyes for a few more minutes. I fall back asleep.

After some time, I hear noises and peer out to see that J has both dogs on their leashes. When she sees me through the open flap, she asks if I want to join them for their walk. "Yes," I say, mainly because this will be our last day together on this adventure. I creep slowly out of the tent; I need a few minutes to completely open my eyes. Once I'm standing in front of the tent, I take Stormy's leash.

"Did they sleep well after we got back?" I ask.

J smiles with a sense of relief in her voice. "Yes—they were really good last night. Everyone had a good night's sleep," she adds.

I look down at them. "Do you know this is your last day on our trip?" I ask Stormy and Striker. Their eyes are inquisitive and their ears are up. They might not understand what I'm saying, but they're ready for their walk. Stormy pulls me forward, and we start walking towards the creek. When we get there, we let them get into the water and splash around even though it's a cold morning.

We return to break down our camp for the last time: stuffing the tent parts into its carrying bag, folding the sleeping bag and chairs and rug, rolling up the yoga mat. All of that goes into the storage carrier along with the remainder of the dog food (which isn't much). We complete this in record time and with a silent cadence. The dogs are quietly lying on the ground and watching us as we finalize our tasks for the ride home, contentedly enjoying their last doggie trip moments amid nature. But pretty soon, it's time to go.

We all get into the van and say goodbye to our campsite and drive out. Before we completely exit the park, we decide to stop at the lodge and pick up coffees for the road. The parking lot is almost full—I pull up next to a large bus with tinted windows at the edge of the lot.

All four of us get out. Several guys are standing in front of the bus, and a few of them inquire about Striker's injury as we walk past. J gives them the standard response and we all chat for a few minutes as the guys pet the dogs. They mention that they stayed at the lodge last night, and we ask them how the accommodations were. "Nice," they say. We have a typical conversation about the many natural wonders of Big Sur. We give them a brief recap of our road trip and then they tell us what they're doing here: music. Apparently, they're in a band. That explains the big bus.

"Which band?" I ask. I can't quite hear the reply, but I shake my head politely and say, "That's great!" From our response, they could tell, we hadn't heard of the band. I'm sure J heard their band name and will tell me the name later. But apparently whoever it was, J wasn't impressed. "Where do you play?" I ask. "Do you ever get down to Los Angeles?"

"Yes," one responds, "we play all over. Actually, we're playing tonight at the Henry Miller Library in Big Sur." *It would have been great to hear some music tonight,* I think, *but we have to return the van today and we have a six-hour drive in front of us. Darn.*

As much as I'd like to keep chatting, we need to get on the road, so I head inside and buy our coffees while J continues talking to them. When I return with our coffees in hand, I regretfully point out that we need to get going. They were the cutest guys we encountered on our entire road trip! Too bad it was the last day on our last stop. We exchange goodbyes and tell them we hope the show goes great later on.

Back in the van, we get ourselves situated for the next few hours: I prepare the playlist set-up, J battens down everything in the back and the dogs jump into their places. I pull the van in drive and we're finally off! We are going home.

Turning left on Hwy 1, we head south along the coast. It's a zigzagging, winding road for miles, picturesque and dramatic. I'm driving slowly, negotiating the sharp curves with both hands tightly clenched on the wheel. Again, this view never gets old, just stunning! The cars in front of us are practically crawling along, the passengers sticking their cell phones outside the windows and tapping away to get photos of the oceanside. There are viewpoints to pull over, but we decide to keep going. It's a long way home and we're tired.

After a couple of hours, we arrive at San Luis Obispo and stop for gas. J gets both dogs out for a quick walk around the station. When we're both back in our seats, J brings up our conversation with the guys at the lodge. "You know those guys back there were Modest Mouse, right?" she asks.

"What??" I say, surprised. I look at her with a big question mark on my face. "Those guys were Modest Mouse?"

"Yes, he said they were Modest Mouse," J says.

My jaw drops, and my mind hurries back to the moment in our conversation when they said their band name, when I couldn't understand what they had said. I replay that moment over and over again… "He said, 'Modest Mouse!'" I scream, throwing my hands up in the air. "Modest Mouse!! Oh, my God!!!"

J starts laughing. "Yes, they were Modest Mouse."

The dogs are startled by my screaming and our laughing. J and I look back at them and say, "It's okay, it's okay," and lower our voices. I'm in shock. I love Modest Mouse! Who within the band were we speaking to? Was the one who told us "Modest Mouse" the lead singer? We are laughing hysterically as I keep repeating, "I love Modest Mouse!!"

J says, "I thought you knew them, but when you didn't say anything, I just left it alone. Let's play some Modest Mouse."

"Yes!" I say excitedly. I pull out onto the road as J picks up my phone and searches for Modest Mouse on my playlist. Nothing there, she says. Strange—I thought I had a bunch of their songs. "I see a bunch of Muse, though," she says.

Oops! I realize I mixed up Muse with Modest Mouse. "Oooohhhh…!" I blurt out. "It's Muse, not Modest Mouse—I love *Muse*—but Modest Mouse is good, too."

We laugh some more. She plays Muse and then searches for Modest Mouse on Spotify and plays a few of their songs. "Oh, yeah!" I exclaim. "I really like this song, too!"

A few hours later

A wall of fatigue hits me as we finally arrive at J's house in Los Angeles. We tumble out, the dogs excited to smell their own house again. As soon as we open the door, they crazily jump and run around: on the sofas, into the backyard, back and forth along the hallway. They know they're home. While the dogs are preoccupied, J and I unpack their belongings.

Before I leave, I give J and the dogs big hugs and kisses. Stormy gets an extra doggie hug—I'm going to miss him. I'm off to drop off the campervan, pick up my car and spend another hour and a half driving home. Ugh! What a long, long day! I can't wait to sleep in a proper bed again.

Two weeks later

Since we left on our road trip, nothing new has happened on the business front—we're still waiting to see if the investors will be able to sell their company in order to invest in ours. Whatever may happen, though, J and I are both in a good place: no anxiety, no "what-if's," no regrets. Each of us is thinking about our next chapter should we need to move on.

J is coming by my house later with the dogs, and I'm looking forward to us spending the evening together. When they arrive, a sense of nostalgia sets in; seeing the dogs warms my heart, unlike any time before. Their tails are wagging—they're excited to see me, too. "Ahhh…" J says. "They're so happy to see their Auntie Mia! They've missed you."

It's a cool, pleasant evening, and we decide to go down to the beach for sunset. I throw on my fleece jacket for the walk. J's got the leashes; I put on Stormy's and then slide my hand into my jacket pocket and pull out a handful of crumpled poop bags. I shout out with a smile, "I still have a bunch from our trip!" We start to go out my front door, but I stop. "Hold on! Let's take a bottle of wine and some cheese for us."

She nods her head yes. "Perfect! And I've brought along my new hula hoop, I'll bring it, too." After our trip, she researched hula hoops and bought a couple online. She's been practicing—Angel (our Yosemite camp neighbor) was her inspiration.

I grab a small cooler and stick in a bottle of rosé, two of the acrylic glasses I purchased at one of the tasting wineries and some leftover cheese from our trip. I smell it first—yup, it's fine. Cooler in one hand and Stormy's leash in the other, I rejoin J and the dogs, and we make our way down to the beach. In another hour, the sun will be setting. Only a few people are nearby and no other dogs, ideal conditions.

"Let's unleash them," J suggests. I happily nod in agreement and unclip Stormy's leash. J does the same with Striker. They both begin running along the water's edge, flying along as if they had wings. Striker has such a strong pace on his three-and-a-half legs, and although Stormy is a little slower on his four, he's just as vibrant, aging soul and all.

We take a seat on the beach blanket I brought with us and watch them play with each other. J gets up and starts swinging her hula. Of course, the dogs come running to us without any hesitation or stopping, throwing sand all over the blanket and interrupting J's rhythmic hula swing. As I get up to clean off some of the sand and re-spread the blanket, I pull out the cheese and wine.

"Can I help?" asks J.

"Yes!" I fondly remember all the times she asked me that while I was preparing dinner. "You can open the bottle and pour us some wine."

Blanket rearranged, we sit and continue to watch the dogs happily run around as we sip our rosé. "How's the dating scene?" J asks. I tell her I've uninstalled the dating app and I'm taking a break. She laughs.

"What will you do if our company folds?" I ask.

She pauses, then says, "I think I'll go to Mexico for a yoga retreat. What would you do?"

"I don't know…Maybe write a book," I say quickly, not giving it much thought.

"What about?"

"How not to date?"

We burst out laughing and then take another sip of wine. But as I think about my answer for a few more seconds, my thoughts quickly turn upbeat. "Maybe I'll write about two girls, two dogs and a campervan," I answer.

The End

—